THE GIRL WHO LOVED DEATH

By
PAUL W. FAIRMAN

I0616780

ARMCHAIR FICTION
PO Box 4369, Medford, Oregon   97501-0168

*For more information about Armchair Books and products, visit our
website at…*

www.armchairfiction.com

Or email us at…

armchairfiction@yahoo.com

DOORWAY TO ANOTHER WORLD...

It was the most baffling set of questions a private eye was ever faced with answering. And the toughest inquiry of the bunch was: How on earth did a normal-sized girl get shrunk down to a pint-sized beauty?

Nick Saturday wasn't really much of a private detective, and he was usually the first one to admit it. But in spite of all his professional shortcomings, he somehow managed to get hired to find a missing dame—a spectacularly gorgeous redhead named Helen Burdette. So—like all good flatfoots—he grabbed a cab and starting combing the streets of the city for her. The problem was that he had the right city and even the right street—but entirely the wrong world!

FOR A COMPLETE SECOND NOVEL, TURN TO PAGE 71

CAST OF CHARACTERS

NICK SATURDAY
An out-of-work detective. When he finally landed a case, he found himself thrust into the most fantastic mystery imaginable.

MIKE CONLIN
He was Saturday's peg-legged landlord and he hired him to find a missing red-head. It was a simple case…or was it?

HELEN BURDETTE
A true mystery woman. The first time Saturday saw her she was completely in the nude—and inside a refrigerator!

WINONA KEATING
This drop-dead gorgeous blonde was an expert in turning on the charm—right before she had your head bashed in.

DR. WILLIAM KINDER
Saturday called on the good doctor to aid a lady in distress, but he probably should have checked his credentials at the door.

SAM KANE
This down-on-his-luck cab driver owed money to an unemployed private eye—and paying it back almost got him killed.

CHAPTER ONE

I WAS SITTING at my shabby desk, in my shabby office, and the accepted manner of a private eye with no cases, when he walked in. He came stiffly, as though on wooden legs, and his mouth was twisted into a permanent leer. My hand stole quietly toward the right top drawer of my desk.

I knew all about my visitor. He walked stiffly because he'd lost both legs in the war and they'd given him a new pair. The leer came from a set of false teeth bought from a bargain dentist, I knew what the guy wanted, too—his rent. It was three months overdue and I didn't have it.

His name was Mike Conlin and he was a pretty good joe. He came and sat down beside my desk, saw me fumbling in the drawer, and offered me one of his—a Chesterfield. I took it gratefully. I said, "If you're looking for excuses, you're going to be surprised. I'm fresh out. No dough—no alibis. No prospects."

He was a man who had suffered a lot. It showed in his eyes. They had that depth found only in the eyes of people who have lived the hard way. Lines came only when he smiled, as he was doing now. He said, "Why don't you give it up, Nick? It's a tough game. I understand even Philip Marlowe and Paul Pine are out of work."

"It's my racket. Can I help it if people are getting too yellow to break the statutes?"

He regarded me pensively for a few moments. I said, "Maybe in a week or so—if things break..."

"I didn't come after any money. It's just that a thing came up—a way we can cut the debit and give you a little practice.

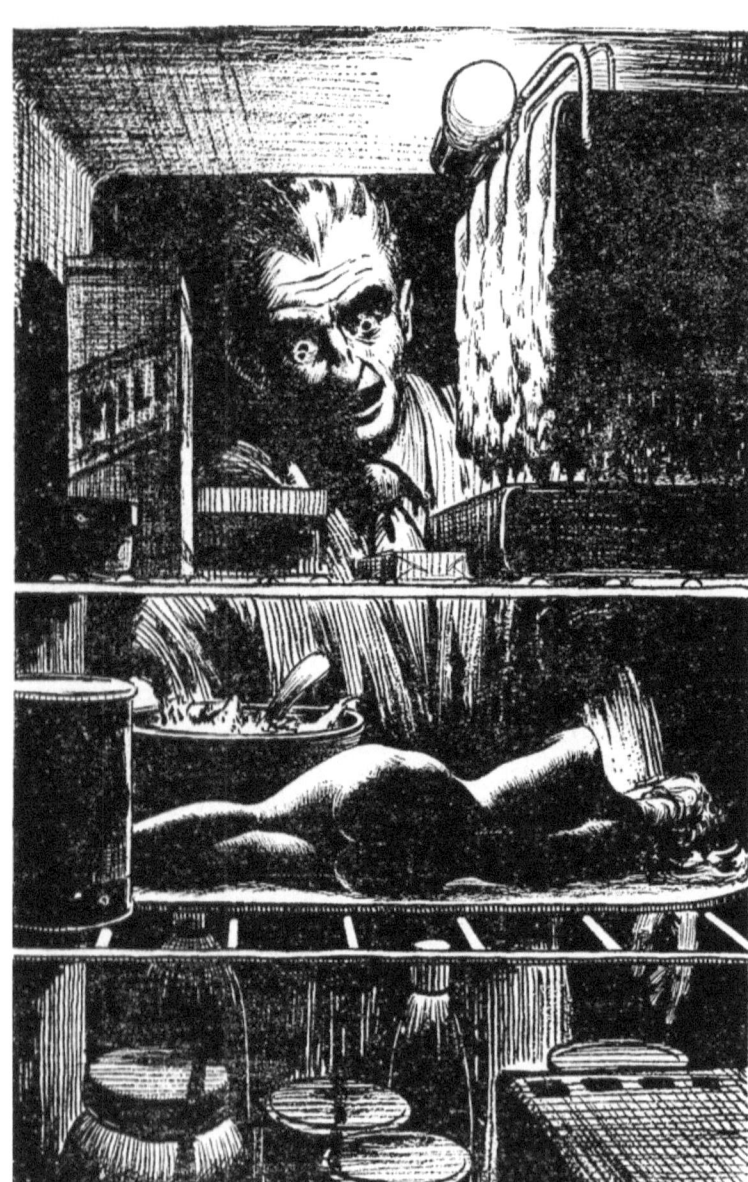

God knows you must need it by now."

I was getting ready to snarl when he took the Chesterfields from his pocket, held one back, and tossed the pack in front of me. How can you snarl at a guy like that? "I'm open for business—even on due-bills. Tell me."

He looked down, slowly, and gazed at the things he walked on. His eyes were wistful. "I had a girl once," he said.

"Quit feeling sorry for yourself."

"I'm not. That's part of it. It was a pre-Korea romance."

"A 'Dear John?'"

"Not exactly. After I got back she came to the hospital twice, but something had gone out of it—something was missing."

I was ready to bark at him again, but I saw that he wasn't punning. He missed the obvious completely.

"I don't think the loss of my legs had anything to do with it. I honestly don't. I'm convinced it would have been the same if I'd come back whole."

It seemed a good thing for him to believe. I said, "You just...kind of drifted apart?"

"That was it. She didn't come again. I left the hospital eventually, but we were out of touch. I didn't try to contact her."

Another silent interlude while I lighted a second cigarette. He watched intently. After I'd taken three drags and it was going well, he said, "Six months passed and I'd done a pretty good job of forgetting her. Then—this morning—there was a little item in the paper."

HE HAD a *Gazette* folded in his side pocket. He took it out, opened it, laid it on my desk, and pointed. "Right there. Evidently not important enough to make the front page, but it knocked all my forgetting into a cocked hat."

I concentrated on the item—a scant inch in a place Mother Mitchell hadn't quite filled with her mouth-tempting recipes:

GIRL DISAPPEARS

Police were today investigating a report that Helen Burdette, 26, of 1126 Weber Place, is missing. The girl resided with her mother, Mrs. Patrice Burdette, 47, a widow. Miss Burdette worked as a stenographer at the Regal Toy Company, 1750 Wilson Avenue. The police are not yet convinced of foul play.

I pushed the paper back across the desk. "Probably stayed with a girl friend."

"Could be," Conlin mused. "Probably nothing sinister about it at all. But I'm in the position of a guy with money to burn—" He grinned fleetingly. "So far as you're concerned, that is. So I'd like to have you look into it. Go over and see Mrs. Burdette—let her know somebody's on her side."

"The girl herself will probably answer the door."

"Could be. In that case we only tear one corner off your rent bill."

I shrugged. "You're the boss—boss. I gather I'm being retained to find one lost, strayed or stolen girl named Helen Burdette. It might cost you a lot. It's a long walk to Weber Place, and my car is in the clutches of the capitalists."

He dug into his pocket and brought out the green paper. He gave me some of it and said, "Fortunately the busses are still running. Let me know when you find out anything—just like in the detective stories."

"Will do."

He took one of the Chesterfields, lit it, and walked carefully out of the office.

I CAUGHT a Lincoln Street bus to a cabstand on Adams and Western. Sam Kane was sitting behind the wheel of his beaten-up hack. He said, "Nick Saturday! As I live and breathe. Great to see you."

"How about the fifty for locating the drunk that—"

"I know—I know, Nick. I been wanting to slip you, but my damage check ain't come through yet. I ain't even got gas money. The wife's been grabbing every cent—"

"Maybe I can take some of it out in trade. Got a little running around to do."

"You got money for gas?"

"Hell, no."

Sam sighed and straightened behind the wheel. "Get in."

He got the hack rolling and pulled into a cut-rate gas station where a fat man in dirty overalls was pulling the rear wheels off an old Chevrolet. Sam got out and went over and braced the fat man. The latter scowled, then came over and shot a tankful of gas into Sam's hack.

After the guy went back to the Chevrolet, Sam got into the hack and said, "I got that repair job for Louie but he's got no dough for commission, so I took it out in gas. Where to, Nick?"

I gave him the Weber Place address and sat back on the ratty cushions feeling like a plutocrat. It really wasn't such a bad world after all. Nobody made any money, but we all got along.

On the way over, I had Sam stop in front of a pawnshop. I went in and used one of Mike Conlin's tens to get my gun out of hock, and then I was ready for business.

That block on Weber Place wasn't good or bad. It lay just about dead center between the two. The address I wanted was a red brick anthill with about fifty cells, according to the directory. I found the one I wanted. Then, from force of habit, I pushed three other buttons. One of them buzzed me in and I walked up to the second floor and found 219 on a neat little white card over another signal button. I pushed the button and waited. Nothing happened. I pushed it again. I could hear the muffled bell beyond the panel, but no one inside did anything about it.

I tried the knob. The door opened. I went inside.

I didn't belong in there, of course, but I've heard tell of Presidents who didn't belong in the White House either, so I didn't let it worry me any.

The door opened directly into a neat but not gaudy living room. The furniture was the kind you buy by the carload to furnish big red brick anthills. The carpeting was bought by the square acre and cut to fit. The artificial fireplace had a gas log in it. The carpet was clean. The place was utterly still.

I called out, "Anybody home?" trying to make it sound real casual and cheery. Nobody answered.

The next logical point of progression was a closed door in the far wall. It could have led into the bathroom, but it didn't. I opened it and saw a bed covered with a pink spread. A woman was sitting on the bed. She wore a green dressing gown and there was something peculiar about her. At her feet was a long cardboard packing box. She was staring down fixedly at it. Yes—something definitely peculiar.

I stepped into the room to make a further investigation and the ceiling fell on my head. I thought it did, anyhow. At least, something fell on my head. It could have been the ceiling or an anvil or a section of a football stadium. Only one point could be taken as a certainty.

Something fell on my head.

WHEN I WOKE up I had two heads. A new one had grown onto the one I'd come in with. I reached up and touched the new one and yelped from the pain. It wasn't a second head. It was only a bump the size of a cantaloupe.

As I opened my eyes, I'd evidently just about ridden out my ten cents' worth, because the merry-go-round slowed down and stopped with a sickening lurch. I didn't have any more money so I got off with the calliope still howling, while they packed up the carnival and moved on to a new town and I was standing in the middle of a quiet bedroom—just another private eye with a bump on his head.

Nothing had changed so far as I could see. The sun was still pouring in the small window. The pink spread was still on the bed. The woman still wore the green dressing gown and hadn't moved an inch. She still sat on the edge of the bed staring down at the box at her feet.

She stared into the box and I stared at her—for a full minute. She could have been a statue—or a frozen body—or a person hypnotized into rigidity. I took a step, forward. Nothing happened. I took another and had myself a long look into the cardboard box. It held a doll. A big doll in a fluffy blue dress. A doll over two-feet long with white shoes and stockings and staring, blue eyes.

But eyes not more fixed nor staring than those of the woman, I stepped close and extended a hand. But I didn't touch the woman. Something stopped me at the last moment. Something told me that if I wanted all hell to break loose, I should touch the woman.

I didn't want all hell to break loose, so I rerouted my hand downward—slowly—very slowly—and picked the doll out of its box.

A beautiful doll. One any four-year-old would burn a house down to come by. But nothing that I could see to turn a grown woman into a staring statue. I went over the doll thoroughly, then bent over and returned it to the box. The woman hadn't flicked an eyelash.

I backed out of the room, carefully, wondering from whence had come the attempt to fracture my skull. Certainly not from the woman on the bed. My eyes had been on her as I'd blacked out. I went to the telephone stand and concentrated on a yellow wall-card that listed various numbers. There was a drugstore, a delicatessen, an undertaker, a garage, a baby-sitting service, and a doctor.

I called the doctor—a William Kinder, M. D. He evidently wasn't a very good doctor—just as I evidently wasn't a very good private eye—because he was sitting in his office waiting for business and said he could come right over.

I WAITED ten minutes, during which time I snooped the joint in approved private eye style—finding any number of things that were none of my business. But if there is anything a private dick thrives on it's a volume of items that are none of his business. I pocketed a few of the more interesting ones.

A card reading: *Hillside Sanatorium for Women-Ellen Kornbloom, R. N.* A corner of the telephone book cover with two names and phone numbers on it: *The Frolics Cafe-State 2-9300*, and the *Regal Toy Company-Placer 4-8086*.

I still had a few minutes left, so I sat down to drag from my mind a little thing that had been worrying me, and give it the once-over.

A small thing, with possibly no foundation whatever, but just before I'd been bopped my eyes had rested on the cardboard box at which the frozen woman had been—and still was—staring. I'd been sure it held a doll, but I was sure also that the doll had been naked. I'd seen expanses of pink skin—certainly no frilly blue dress. Another impression—one of which I was not sure enough to mention before witnesses, but which plagued me nonetheless—that it had been an obscene doll; one you wouldn't give your little girl for Christmas.

But this last was so vague in my memory, I was forced to

charge it off as illusion. I was sure enough of the other point, however, to give it thought—to build from it. If I was right, some joker had waited for me behind the door—had slugged me and then put a nice blue dress on a naked doll and had gone off about other business.

This seemed pretty silly. Why would the lack of a dress on a doll kindle the urge in some party to knock my brains out? I couldn't figure it. Then the buzzer sounded and I opened the door.

For what came in I could have called Central Casting in Hollywood rather than a local number. He was short, pale, and wore black shoes and had a meticulous black Van Dyke. He asked, "Did you call for a doctor?" I said I had, and he wanted to know where the patient was. I led him toward the bedroom.

He took two steps inside and stopped, staring. If he'd had a tail to go with the beard, he'd have passed for a prize bird dog on point.

Now he tiptoed forward and peered down into the frozen woman's face. He looked at her from several angles but kept his hands off her. Then he turned and tiptoed out into the living room. I followed him.

He said, "We've got to get through to the fire department immediately." The inhalator squad carries a straitjacket. We're going to need it."

HE PUT the call through, then dropped into a chair and wiped his face with a snowy handkerchief. I sat down opposite him. I asked, "What do you think is wrong with her, Doctor?"

He replaced the handkerchief in his breast pocket. "Shock of some sort. It's not epilepsy. Some sort of terrific shock. Her static condition can't last much longer. I hope they get here in time with that straitjacket. There'll be trouble when she comes out of it."

"What do you think caused it?"

He shrugged. "I haven't the least idea. I haven't even got a history of the patient. Does she have a family doctor?"

"I don't know."

This centered his interest on me. "You didn't give me your name over the phone."

I told him also why I was there.

The doctor thought it over. "From the posture and the intensity of the shock, I'd say the cause of her condition was something other than the daughter's disappearance."

"The doll?"

"That hardly seems logical either. Shock is a tricky thing, though. Sight of the doll, coupled with thoughts of her daughter—"

"But you don't believe that did it...do you?"

"No." Kinder glanced nervously toward the bedroom door. You could tell he didn't like what was inside.

I said, "If you're afraid she'll come to, how about giving her a shot? I'll try to hold her and you can work fast."

He shook his head. "We'd better ride out our luck and hope they get here in time."

They came pretty fast—two young men in white coats, one carrying a canvas bundle, the other a black bag similar to that of Doctor Kinder.

Kinder introduced himself, then turned to me. "What about relatives—nearest of kin?"

"I don't know of any."

He thought that over before he said, "Well, let's get it over with."

We went into the bedroom. Kinder opened his bag and filled a hypodermic. He motioned me back. "These men are experienced in handling cases like this. You stand by. I'll yell if we need you."

They knew their business. They moved in on the woman from either side. They made me glad I hadn't touched her because, at first contact she came up off the bed like a steel spring. But they were ready. They took quick holds on her after a manner of long experience. One of them even had a hand to spare. He used it to stifle an animal scream that welled up from her taut throat.

Kinder was no amateur, either. He latched onto her right arm and got the hypo in and out before she even felt it. Then he grabbed the straitjacket and the three men—working as a machine—got her into it.

It was really needed, because the shot didn't take effect for almost five minutes. During that time they kept her under control, working as gently as possible. When she passed out, they stepped back and wiped their faces.

"You'll take her to the County Hospital?" I asked.

Kinder glanced up at me, nodding. "It's customary. The police will start a routine search to locate relatives. If you find any, you might let them know."

They carried Mrs. Burdette to a black ambulance in the street and drove away.

Sam was asleep behind the wheel of his hack. I nudged him awake and we headed back toward my office. When we got there Sam looked at the meter and said, "I owe you $6.40 less than I did. You want me to wait, or can I go out and try to make a buck?"

"I'll pick you up at the stand when I want you. So long."

CHAPTER TWO

MIKE CONLIN lived in three rooms on the third floor. I went up and knocked on his door; I could hear him coming. He opened the door and said, "My left leg's squeaking like hell. I'll have to oil it. Come on in."

I went in and he cracked a bottle and I took two stiff drinks.

"Any progress to report?"

I shook my head. "Haven't even got started yet. There were interruptions." I sat down with a third shot in my paw and told him.

He listened to the whole thing. When I'd finished he said, "I didn't expect it to be easy. I've got a hunch Helen's in real trouble. Poor Mrs. Burdette."

"I don't get it. How could a doll set a woman off like that? It doesn't make sense."

Mike looked up quickly. "How much rent did you owe me?"

"Two hundred and a quarter."

"We're going to forget about that. Call it a three-month concession. We'll start from scratch—right now."

"Why the generosity?"

"I want you to go ahead with this and I want your best. Under that setup I don't think I could get it. I think men work better for money than for anything else. What's your regular fee?"

I told him. Fifteen dollars a day and expenses. He forked out some more bills. "There's three hundred. When that's gone, let me know. I don't care how much you spend. I want action."

I thought it over for a minute before I said, "Look—I think you're making a mistake."

"How so?"

"Maybe I'm not the right man for you."

"I don't follow."

"Maybe I'm not the smartest private dick in town, and you can afford the best. I'm rough and I'm tough. My face proves that. It's been hit with everything but a Cadillac crankcase. That doesn't make me smart, though. You can hire a lot of guys who don't get behind in their rent."

He looked at me for a surprised moment, then grinned. "Thanks for giving me the chance, but I'll take you. I like tough mugs. They win wars. Brains are a dime a dozen. Get going."

I said, "Okay—you're paying the bills." I got up and started for the door.

Mike said, "I wish you'd go over to the County right away and check on Mrs. Burdette. See that she gets the best. I've had a hunch any relatives you find aren't going to help with the bills."

"Okay—I'll let you know."

I went downtown first and got my Pontiac roadster out of hock. Now I had my gun and my car and almost two hundred bucks in my pocket. Enough to lick the world. I headed for the County Hospital.

A SMALL pretty blonde was in the receiving room, but the pleasantness was offset by the presence of a large, horse-faced brunette who was homely and seemed to be glad of it. I asked for Mrs. Burdette's ward number.

The blonde began rifling through a card index. The brunette snorted, "Ambulance chaser?"

I said, "Uh-huh. Bad arches. I have to work inside."

The brunette snorted again. The blonde looked up. "When was she admitted?"

"She just came in. Couldn't have been more than an hour."

"Sorry. We have no listing."

"Maybe it's not recorded yet."

"It would be. Listings are made immediately."

"What type of case?" the brunette wanted to know.

This cheered me because I didn't know she cared. "Psychiatric, probably," I told her.

This was grounds for a fresh snort. "She wouldn't be registered here. Psycho is Building B. Separate."

I thanked the blonde and went through the main building to the smaller one back by the morgue, marked B. An ex-football husky held down the desk in there. He asked, "Looking for somebody, chum?" His manner showed he was a political appointee and proud of it.

I told him.

He shook his head. "You got the wrong nut shop. Nobody's been brought in here all day."

"Maybe there's another door."

He scowled. "Wise guy, huh? Listen, they cart 'em in past me or not at all."

"Okay, bub—I just asked." I turned and walked out. It wasn't that I doubted him. I just couldn't dope it. Or maybe it was my inferiority complex.

I crossed the street to a one-arm and got a cup of coffee. I sat there nursing it—thinking. Fine thing. I'd been hired by a nice guy to do a job. The guy had given me money and everything. He'd asked me to find a girl. Not unreasonable whatever way you looked at it. Now I'd have to go back to him and tell him that I wasn't making any progress. In fact I was going backwards. I just lost the girl's mother.

I was damned if I would. I went out and got into the

roadster and kited north. There were some men I had to see, and the first on my list was Dr. William Kinder.

THE RED brick apartment building was still there. That hadn't disappeared. I passed it on the way to the address I remembered from the yellow card—Kinder's address. The doc had a second-floor walkup about six blocks away. There were worn gold letters on his window. I went up and found the waiting-room door unlocked. Inside were an old cane lounge, a few ancient magazines, and a sign on an inner door: *Back in an hour.* I tried the inner door. It was locked.

The outer door opened and a mousey little woman came in. She gave me a mousey smile and asked in a squeaky voice, "You wanted to see the doctor?"

I nodded.

"He should be back any minute. I work in the insurance office next door and kind of look after things for him. He got a call over two hours ago, so he should be back soon."

"It isn't important that I wait, if I can just talk to him. Maybe I can call him at the place he went. Did he leave a phone number?"

"No, I'm afraid not."

"An address?"

The woman evidently didn't want Doc Kinder to lose any business. She tried to cooperate. "No, but it was somewhere on Weber Place. Not very far away. I'm sure if you'll just wait—"

I registered a little doubt. "It's a business matter. I may not even have the right man. The Kinder I'm after is very short. He wears a black Van Dyke beard—"

This was a disappointment to the girl. "No. Doctor Kinder is over six feet. He has white hair—no beard."

"Then I've made a mistake. Sorry." I got out as soon as I could and headed for Weber Place. It was dusk now, and the streetlights had been turned on. I parked in front of 1125 and stood for a minute looking up at the building.

There's an old set of instructions about how to find a lost cow. You walk out of the barn, figure you're a cow, and decide where you'd go if you wanted to get lost. I twisted it around a little. I figured I was a doctor walking into the building, and tried to dope out the procedure of anyone who might want me to get lost.

Tracing back, it added up this way. There had been some very fast work by some very fast people. I'd called a doctor these people didn't want to show up. But when Kinder walked into the building, how could they have known who he was and where he was going? There could have been only one way and I went upstairs to verify it.

I LET MYSELF into the Burdette apartment with a piece of celluloid on my key ring. The place was still, lonely, deserted. After making sure of that, I started looking for the bug. It didn't take long to find it. The mike was fastened underneath the telephone table. The wire went down the table leg and out the same hole as the phone wires at the baseboard.

I went back to the front door and checked the layout. The doctor had been taken inside the building or out in the street. Nerve was required in either case, but an inside job looked to me to be the safest. The doc hadn't rung the bell—something I had a right to figure he'd do—so that meant he'd been nailed in the outer lobby. Then he'd either been taken back outside to a waiting car, or been brought in.

The presence of the bug made me favor the latter, but I wasn't ready to barge ahead yet. There was something else that needed thinking out, so I leaned against the lobby wall and tried to puzzle it through.

When I'd first entered Mrs. Burdette's bedroom she'd

been staring down at a box with a naked doll in it. I'd been bopped, and when I'd come to I'd found a doll with a dress on. Evidently something of importance hinged on the doll. Then why hadn't my slugger walked away with the whole thing? Why put a dress on a doll and leave it there?

Obviously the bopper felt it couldn't be removed safely. Why? Because it would be missed. Someone else knew it was there and the scene shouldn't be changed. So the guy who slugged me put a dress on the doll.

He did? Like hell! There'd been something else in that box. The doll had been substituted. Obviously, some person or persons unknown had been in the apartment when I'd arrived. I'd been slugged to keep me from seeing what was in the doll box. Maybe I'd interrupted the switching of the contents.

Anyhow, they probably hadn't expected me to turn up, hadn't known whom I was, and had kept one foot on base, waiting to see which way I'd jump. I called a doctor, which— from their point of view—was evidently the wrong thing to do, so they moved fast. They snatched the doc, sent in their own character who had called their musclemen, and they'd staged a kidnapping right under my big fat nose.

All of which was pretty disgusting from my point of view. Nick Saturday—private eye! It was amazing how I could figure things out after it was too late. But at least I could take it from there.

I went inside and looked things over. The inner lobby fed into a long hallway pointing straight to the rear of the building. It was lined with doors. I walked down the hall. Any one of those apartments could have been the rat's nest I was looking for. But maybe there was a way to narrow it down.

I counted six doors on the right side. Allowing for the elevator, that should have put me directly under the Burdette apartment. The logical spot from which to bug the place.

A CARD on the door panel said, *Winona Keating.* I punched the button. It buzzed inside but didn't bring any footsteps. I buzzed again. Obviously the buzzer wasn't going to bring any footsteps. I leaned against the wall and debated my future. If I snicked the lock and entered, the state could shorten my time of liberty by quite a stretch. Or I might get away with it.

I had never been in jail. I had four convictions to go before they could make it permanent. I tried the knob, pushed back the bolt with my celluloid jimmy, and gave the door a shove.

The lights were on but no one seemed to be around. I stood on the threshold waiting for the silence to break. It didn't. But this was the place I wanted. From the doorway, I could see a pair of earphones lying beside a small recorder. And on the floor beside them was a box containing a big doll wearing a fluffy blue dress.

I went inside and pushed the door shut. At one end of the room an archway showed a small kitchen, complete with refrigerator, stove and sink. I moved in that direction, for no other reason than the necessity of moving somewhere. I began opening doors. The pantry-closets. Nothing of interest. I'd just opened the icebox and gotten a chill, when a phone jangled in the living room.

I closed the refrigerator and stood there wondering whether or not to answer it. It rang again. Two long rings—then a third—and I was turning toward the living room, when someone beat me to it. A door beyond range of my vision opened and a blonde—a very annoyed blonde—came from the bedroom.

She'd evidently just stepped out of the bathtub. She wore a bath towel around her waist and nothing else. And she was angry. She snatched up the phone and barked hello with marked hostility. Then the party at the other end must have identified himself, because she sneered, "Oh, it's you! Good Lord! Can't a girl take a bath? Doorbells ring—phones ring!"

From there on I heard one side of the conversation from which I tried to fill in the other half: "I don't know. I didn't answer it. A peddler probably... I don't know what you're worried about. Everything went off all right... The Sanatorium, of course... What made you think you'd find him here? You might try the club..." The pause was longer this time. It ended when the girl said, "It's in the refrigerator. And I want it gotten out of here. You can send it along with the next load... Two more, I think, but if we can't get them we'll ship without them... Look—I'm wet—I'm getting cold... What?... The two are named Maizie King and Jenny Davis... At the club... Tonight... Goodbye."

She slammed up the phone, still frowning, and went back as she'd come, whipping off the towel as she vanished through the bedroom door.

She didn't close it, though, and I became conscious of the sound of running water in the bathroom beyond. I stood there watching the door. As long as it remained open I had no chance of getting out unobserved. I could see into the bathroom from where I stood. The girl was toweling herself vigorously now, and her anger had not subsided. Scowling darkly, she stood with her feet braced—far apart—and sawed the towel across her back. I waited, wondering why she had to stand full face. While she did so I was helpless unless I wanted to be turned up and, as yet, I didn't. Then, as though obeying my unspoken wish, she dropped the towel, turned and began washing the ring off the bathtub. Three long steps and I had my hand on the refrigerator door.

I OPENED it slowly, to muffle the snap of the lock. It seemed an hour before the door was clear and I could pull it open. A light flashed on inside and I remember hoping the door shielded it from the living room. Then I forgot about the door, the living room, the blonde—everything else—except what I saw lying on the shelf.

I knew instantly that it couldn't have been a doll, although it would have fit perfectly into the box out by the telephone table. I went cold all over, and even if a gun had been pointed at my head I couldn't have taken my eyes off the girl in the refrigerator.

I reached out and touched the body—the perfect little two-foot body—with one finger. The flesh was cold, but soft, yielding, and human. She lay on her back, her little arms straight down her sides. The red hair was perfect, in miniature, as was the face and the exquisite body. All my mental processes had stopped, except an idle flow of consciousness that, I guess, doesn't stop under any circumstances. And I thought: Nick Saturday—a fine private eye. Even when he locates a missing person they can't be normal. When he finds the girl, she's only two feet high and she's lying unconscious in somebody's ice box.

Then some semblance of sanity returned to tell me this wasn't Helen Burdette, even though the face and hair perfectly matched the picture on Mrs. Burdette's dresser signed "Helen, with love."

This was a doll. One of those new dolls with skin that looks human—feels human. They're very clever about things like that these days. But all the time I knew it wasn't true. The flesh was real. And even if such perfect imitation was possible, no one would make a doll with every bodily detail meticulously copied. There is a point beyond which such duplication does not go.

I laid my hand on the flesh. Every sense I possessed told

me the hand was lying on the body of a cold, unconscious, naked girl. I drew it back, shuddering.

THE CLICK of high heels from the bedroom brought me out of it. I closed the door. The lock snapped. The clicking of the heels stopped also.

"Who's there? Who's out there?"

I slid along the wall and stoop with my back pressed hard against the stucco paint job just inside the archway. The blonde didn't make any further inquiries. Instead, the heels clicked across the bedroom, sounded softly on the living room carpet, and then she breezed past me into the kitchenette.

She'd changed the towel for a pair of pink panties, and she had on sheer nylons held up by garters, but she still hadn't done anything about the upper expanses. She turned and saw me.

I couldn't think of anything original to say, so I said, "Good evening," and got set for whatever might come my way.

"Who the hell are you?"

"The name is Nick Saturday."

"What are you doing here?"

"I'm in a pretty shoddy business. I go a lot of places I'm not supposed to—like into people's ice boxes."

I kept waiting for her to realize how she was dressed—or rather, wasn't dressed—and to do something about it. At least fold her arms. But she evidently had more important things to worry about. Quick fear washed across her face. I could tell that she had a fast mind and that it was probably going faster than it had ever gone before. I could almost see various plans of procedure flash into her consciousness and then go into discard.

Suddenly she smiled. "Well, as long as you're here I guess

there's nothing I can do about it. Do you mind if I get some clothes on—or did you have other plans?"

It was amazing how pleasantly curved that previously sullen mouth could become. Surprising how she could take six simple words and give them such a tone of happy anticipation.

"You'd better get some clothes on," I said.

She pouted prettily. "If you say so." She walked past me with a sidelong glance calculated to melt me down and bog me in my own tallow.

It almost did, but not quite. I came out of it just as she disappeared into the bedroom. I dived after her. I can move fast, once I make up my plodding mind, and I moved just fast enough to clamp a hand over her wrist as she dragged an automatic out of her dressing-table drawer.

"You SOB," she said frankly. "If you think you're going to get away with this—"

I DON'T think she expected me to stand there and let her kill me, and I made industrious efforts to keep her from doing it. As I grabbed, I wished she'd had clothes on. Her nakedness put me at a disadvantage. I'd had a Christian upbringing, and this made for a certain restraint where a nude girl was concerned.

But Christianity doesn't teach suicide, and the girl meant business. It was no time to be a gentleman, so I took hold of her.

She didn't play fair. She fought like a man until she found it didn't help. Then she began fighting like a woman. She said, "Take your hands off me! Haven't you got any decency?"

"Just as much as the next guy, baby, but survival comes first."

Now she played a really low-down, dirty trick. Suddenly

she went limp in my arms and a peculiar light dawned in her blue eyes; an odd expression came to her face. It was an expression that—had it been other than phony—Freud could have explained because he made such things his life work. The girl's lips parted slightly; she looked up into my face as though she'd discovered something there—or something within herself—that was too overpowering to be denied.

Her eyes, her mouth, her body said that she no longer cared for anything but the demands of the moment. She twisted around. Her arms encircled my neck. Her mouth smashed against mine.

I didn't believe it, but I'm not made of stone, and it held me—held me long enough for the party who'd tiptoed into the room to get close enough for the business. A second later I got the business right across the skull. As I went down and out, a vagrant, silly thought flashed through my mind: *Man, how that girl can kiss.*

CHAPTER THREE

I WAS lying on a bed in a square, white room. I was wearing slacks and undershirt. I didn't feel like Nick Saturday or anybody else I knew, and I had the idea a great deal of time had passed since the gorgeous blonde had kissed me and sent me *here*—wherever here was. A cluster of bulbs in the center of the ceiling shot pitiless white rays down into my eyes.

I turned my head and saw the hypo punctures in my right arm below the shoulder. The arm was lumpy and purple. I knew I was all doped up.

But this seemed only of passing interest. The interesting thing was the guy I'd turned out to be. I wasn't Nick Saturday. I was some character I'd have to talk to and get acquainted with.

Saturday was quite a guy himself. A guy who went around and found women frozen with fear staring into doll boxes; who opened refrigerators and found cute little two-foot redheads relaxing on ice; who chummed with blondes who wore bath towels and handed out skull-splitting kisses.

Quite a guy, but nobody at all beside this new jerk who watched the ceiling light turn into a blonde without even a towel on and thought nothing of it.

I sat up and got deathly sick. The room felt like it was on coasters and the ride was free. I hung on as we all went around a bend. Then it was over and I staggered to a dripping washbowl in the far corner and listened to the droplets intone a monotonous ditty: sucker for a sap! Sucker for a sap!

I strangled the faucet. It gurgled and spat water. Blessed stuff, water. You could gulp it down by the bucketful. You could get high on it.

I drank a bucketful and got high. The binge carried me back toward bed. Then it vanished and I really got sick. I dived for the bed and missed it. I landed on the floor and sat there with my legs crossed like an Indian brave dreaming of the Great White Father's scalp. I sat there in the middle of a square white room and crooned to myself:

"I'm Nick Saturday. I've been slugged and booted and shot full of dope. I love all mankind and I'm not very bright and I like to get along with people, but by God somebody's going to pay.

"That above all. To hell with cold little redheads and big, hot blondes. To hell with the respect of the decent element. Somebody's going to pay."

I GOT up and went to the door and turned the knob. It didn't open. That hurt me. It meant I wasn't trusted. I was an apprentice upon whom the eye of suspicion rested. When you turn knobs, doors should open. It hurt me deeply.

But I laughed through my pain. Nick Saturday had a way with locks. That day when they mislaid the keys to Fort Knox they called in Nick and he opened the vault for them. Then he turned down the gold brick they offered him, because he knew they couldn't spare it.

Full of dope and nutty as an old English Christmas cake.

I floated around the room, looking here and there for whatever I could find. There had to be something. Some little thing in this bare room to pick a lock with.

I found it: a nail in the moulding someone had once hung a picture on. I stood on the washbowl and pried the nail out. Then I spent some time bending it just so. It hurt my fingers but it was a labor of love and I didn't mind.

So I took the little bent nail and opened the great big door and went out into the hall. It was a quiet, narrow hall. A nice respectable hall that shushed people like me. I refused to be shushed. Then I caught on. The hall was my friend. It said, be smart. Open your big yap and you'll get clouted. I winked at the hall, we were pals, and I wondered how things were going in Glocamora. At the same time I wondered how screwy you can get and stay perpendicular. Nick Saturday— crazier than fourteen hatters and somebody was going to pay.

I tiptoed down the hall armed with a machine gun and a demolition bomb. I wondered if I should go back for the spiked knuckle-dusters but decided against it. I approached a partially open door and peeped craftily inside.

There was a bed and a lazy wisp of smoke rising from a cigarette held between the fingers of the man on the bed. I didn't know what his name was but I knew what he'd called himself during our last brief contact. William Kinder, M.D. Now he was lying on the bed reading a paper and taking his ease.

I stepped into the room. I looked down at the man. I

said, "Good evening, you needle-chinned son-of-a-bitch. How do you want it?"

The man jerked to a sitting position, then came to his feet. The fear in his face was balm to my soul. I yelled. "On guard, you scummy freak!" and dove in to annihilate him.

I began with a bone crushing right to his jaw. But something was wrong. It tapped lightly against his cheek and then the man with the black Van Dyke took me by the arm and sat me down on the bed and I couldn't do anything about it.

He yelled, "Tate! Cooper! Come here immediately."

It didn't take them long. They still wore the same white coats they'd used in the Weber Place kidnapping. They still looked like clean-cut, hardworking internees.

"You boys are slipping," the phony Kinder snapped. "Patients wandering around the sanatorium at will. You're slipping badly.

They were chagrined. One of them said, "I'll use straps this time. He won't bother you again."

Kinder brushed his sleeve. "See that he doesn't."

THEY CARRIED me away like an empty sack and put me back in the room. One of them said to the other, "You fool. You forgot to throw the bolt. Get the straps and tie him down. I'm going to finish my coffee."

They went out and the bolt slammed into place. I giggled and circled the room. The windows were locked and barred. Why hadn't I thought of the windows before? I opened one of them and looked out. I was only on the second floor but beyond, under a big yellow moon, was deep, dark wooded land. No houses. No use yelling. Besides, anyone who could hear was probably used to people yelling out these windows.

I heard someone giggling, but I didn't have to look to see who it was. I knew. Nick Saturday, the superman with the creampuff punch. I went back and began examining the bed. It was an interesting bed, full of possibilities. It had four solid legs. Iron legs. The legs on the bed were separate pieces—screwed on. I went to work on one set of screws. I cut my fingers and licked off the blood and maybe the blood gave me strength, because by the time footsteps sounded out in the hall, I had one loose.

The bolt outside rattled and the knob turned. I concentrated on the door. Timing did it. Timing makes champions in golf, tennis and bed-leg-swinging. I brought the iron leg back over my shoulder and stood poised. The door opened. I started my swing.

A head appeared. The guy was being cautious. He'd seen that the bed was empty and he thought I might be hanging from the chandelier waiting to throw peanuts at him.

All he saw was the iron leg coming around in an arc. He got his mouth open to scream but the leg was coming fast. It came down against his skull and kept right on going. His skull folded over it.

I PULLED him inside and searched him. He had a gun in his hip pocket. A little .32. A baby gun probably used for shooting mosquitoes off bald patient's heads. I put it in my pocket. He had a bunch of keys. I took those too. I was ready to check out.

I went into the hall. I was feeling better now. The hall didn't shush me and I didn't wink at it.

With partial sanity there came an urge to talk to the little guy with the beard. I went back to his room and peeked in. He'd finished reading the paper and was lying there looking at the ceiling with his hands behind his head. I stepped inside and said, "Yoo-hoo. Guess who's back."

He whirled, came to a sitting posture. I timed a right to connect with his beard just as he came perpendicular. This time it had some power. It snapped his head back and sent him down on the bed.

"One yap out of you and I'll feed you from this heater. It'll mess you up pretty from two feet away." He wasn't a brave man, and so he did what he was told.

He lay there looking up at me with a face full of fear. I liked that. He said, "What do you want?"

I said, "Well I'll be damned! You've been in on this game of footsie from the start, and you ask me what I want. I want some talk—*talk*. The answer to some questions."

He gulped and said nothing.

"I think first I want to know about a two-foot, redheaded girl in the refrigerator. And don't ask me which refrigerator. I'm in no mood."

"I don't know what you're talking about."

I guess I was a different Nick Saturday, even with part of my mind back. The old one had always given people the edge, always given the break, and maybe that's why he'd never gotten anything but a kick in the teeth. Anyhow, I grabbed little Van Dyke by the back of the head, raised my knee, and smashed his face against it.

He let out a garbled squall. I slapped him across the mouth and said, "Shush! You ain't felt nothing yet. I asked a question."

"You wouldn't understand. It's very technical."

"Try me."

"It was one—one of the reduced specimens. They are shipped to—to another place, and weight is important. So long as we have the machinery to reduce them—"

Somebody was standing behind me. Some newfound instinct told me this. And I had the sudden thought it was the party who made a career of swatting me on the skull.

I whirled around. It was the other white-coated muscleman with a sap raised high in his right hand.

I SHOT him in the belly. The .32 made a snapping noise, like an angry Pekinese. The thug's eyes widened accusingly. I wasn't playing fair. I'd had no right to turn around. I shot him again, bringing the arm down and doubling him over himself. He dropped the sap. I picked it up and slugged him. Then I pocketed the gun, grabbed Kinder by the necktie and put a lump dead center on his skull—right on the part in his hair. He slumped down and I went away from there.

Back in the hall I almost became my old self in that I didn't know quite what to do. Call the cops and have this bug's nest fumigated? How could I make my charges stand up? The only evidence I had was a pincushion arm, and this wasn't the only place in town that carried pins. Besides, there was a dead man down the hall. If I didn't prove my case I'd be over a barrel.

I couldn't afford that. I had too many things to do—too many people to find. Too many screwy angles to find answers for. I decided to get out of the place. But, like MacArthur, I sternly told the world I'd be back.

This was a pretty-good-sized joint and I certainly wouldn't be able to travel through it very long without meeting inquiry and resistance. I only hoped I could stretch my luck to the point of finding some clothes. The white slacks and undershirt weren't for the street.

I went back to the room with the three-legged bed and measured my dead jailer for size. He was as I had remembered him—about my build. I took his pants and the white shirt he wore under his white jacket. These would get me by. I started in search of an exit.

There were elevators, but I went through a door marked with a red exit sign and found a stairway. It took me to the first floor. I found a rear door, but it was big and solid, and it had a padlock on it. I didn't have time to fuss with padlocks, so I decided to risk the front.

A large pleasant room with a sort of reception desk on one side had to be crossed. A uniformed nurse sat at the desk, reading the kind of a magazine uniformed nurses at night desks like to read. I walked toward her. She raised her head and looked me over. She didn't jump up and click her heels, nor did she yell murder rape and arson. She just looked. When I got abreast of her, she asked, "Where are you going?"

"I think you're entirely right," I said, "and don't let them tell you different." I opened the door and walked out into the dark night, glad that it was night and happy that it was dark.

I WONDERED where I was. I went to the curb and turned to look back. A plate on a cement post by the walk read: *Hillside Sanatorium for Women*. I'd suspected as much, even though I hadn't seen any women to speak of in the place.

I walked to the nearest corner and read the street sign. Henderson Street and Merrill Avenue. That didn't mean a thing. On down the line I could see brighter lights indicating a business street. I walked toward it.

A cruising cab came by before I'd gone a block and I hailed it. Somehow the look of the cab made me happy. I said, "Take me to 1125 Weber Place. I've got to pick up a doll." I didn't tell him the doll was in a refrigerator and he didn't ask me.

We got there. He pulled down the flag and said, "Two eighty-five."

That made me wonder if I had any money. I dug into the pants I was wearing and found a small wad of bills. I pulled them out without a qualm. The guy who owned them wouldn't need them. There were several fives, some ones, and a ten. I gave the hacker a five and went into the red brick building.

It was a nice building and I was beginning to love it. It was a little like home. Regardless of what they did to me I always came back to the red brick building for more. I went inside and pushed three buzzers and somebody let me through the inner door. I went to the second floor and found the entrance I wanted. I pushed the buzzer with one hand and took my toy pistol out with the other. It made me feel big and strong and independent. So much so that when nobody answered I hit the door with my shoulder. It was as flimsy as I'd expected it to be. It snapped open with scarcely a complaint. I went in and pushed it shut after me.

CHAPTER FOUR

SAM KANE, my favorite hacker, was lying in the middle of the floor, trussed up like a pig on the way to a Chinese market.

He'd been walloped around quite some. One eye was closed. His nose had a starboard list and the gag in his mouth was red.

I took the gag out first. He said, "Damn it all to hell. You got me in trouble."

I went after the knots. "How so?"

"A couple of lugs hired my hack. They put a gun in my neck and brought me here. They wanted to know all about you. When I couldn't tell them anything, they used me for practice."

"They must have seen you on our first trip over."

"I wouldn't be surprised," he growled as he sat up and rubbed his wrists.

"What did they want to know?"

"Everything."

"How much did you remember?"

"Nothing."

"Not even that I'm a private eye?"

"I didn't know that." The grin hurt so he straightened his face. "I wasn't trying to protect you. It was just the principal of the thing—how they went about it. If they'd have offered me a five spot I'd have even told them about your old man's hernia."

"He got that fixed," I said. "Did they take anything out of the refrigerator when they left?"

"I wouldn't know. I was catching up on my sleep about that time."

I headed for the kitchen. He followed me. "Where the hell have you been?"

"In a hospital. I took the dope cure." The two-foot redhead was gone. I'd figured she would be.

"What hospital? What dope cure?"

"The Hillside Sanatorium. The cure made me violent. I left a stiff, a bellyache, and a busted skull. I sure wowed them at the Hillside."

"How about talking sense?"

"There isn't any sense to this thing, but we're going to keep on hitting it left of center until something happens."

"What do you mean *we?*"

"You and me—us. You'd like to get your dukes on the rough-house boys, wouldn't you?"

"I wouldn't mind at all."

I didn't tell him they'd already been gotten to. I said, "We're going to split up for a while. I want you to case a place called the Regal Toy Company. That's the outfit Helen Burdette worked for."

"Who's Helen Burdette?"

"The girl I'm looking for. I'll tell you about it when I get time."

"That'll be nice. What for do I case this joint?"

"Just go over and get the lay. Come to my place in the morning and I'll have something worked out."

"Where you going in the meantime?"

"To a night club. The Frolics Cafe."

"Why?"

"To get a drink."

Sam looked exasperated. "You go to the toy joint. I'll go to the club and get the drink."

"It wouldn't work out right. Let's get out of here."

As we left the building I wondered where my blonde was. I wondered what she'd look like with a blouse on. I wondered what the hell this was all about. I said, "Give me your jacket. I'll need it."

"What for?"

"They won't let me into the Frolics in my shirt sleeves."

Sam complied grudgingly. "You got clean shorts on? Mine's fresh from this morning."

"Don't be so bitter."

"And another thing, I know where you can find at least one of the monkeys that worked me over."

I got into the front seat of the hack beside Sam. "Where?"

"He was sore about something. Said he was going back to Timate."

"Back to where?"

"Timate was what he said."

"How do you spell it?"

"How the hell do I know? T-i-m-a-t-e, I guess."

"Never heard of it. A suburb someplace?"

"You got me. Maybe it's another town."

"Did the guy talk with an accent?"

"Uh-uh. Not that I noticed."

"I thought maybe it was another country."

Sam growled, "It'd be just like the rat to skip out without his lumps. Here's the Frolics."

"Okay. Drop over in the morning."

Sam clashed his gears. "Casing a toy factory. Of all the lousy—"

That was all I heard as I walked into the Frolics.

IT WAS a typical glitter joint with ankle-deep carpets and lots of gilt paint. On the bandstand a band of cats were combing various expressions of agony out of some finance company's instruments. I went to the bar and ordered Scotch with plain water—no ice.

I nursed it awhile, the barkeep being busy. Pretty soon he wandered over and I had him pour me another. I asked, "How about you?"

He glanced around. "I'll pour one under the bar. Drink it later."

"Okay. Jenny around?"

"Jenny who?" he asked, but not with any belligerence.

"Davis. An old friend of mine. Thought I might say hello to her. Heard she was working here."

"Can't place the name. One of the ponies, maybe."

I let it rest for a minute until he said, "Is it important?"

"Not especially. Just thought I'd ask."

"If it's worth a couple of bucks I could find out." When I didn't say anything he went on: "The money's for the porter. Them guys wouldn't slap your back if you was choking, unless they got paid."

I pushed a five out of my change pile on the bar. "Whatever you can save is yours."

He took the bill and went to the end of the bar. Pretty soon a porter came by and they huddled for a minute and then the porter went away.

I waited ten or fifteen minutes. The band didn't learn anything in that length of time. They kept right on playing badly. People came and went. The bar filled and emptied. A voice behind me asked, "Were you looking for me?"

I turned. She was small, dark, and cute. She wore an orange dress and had some kind of an orange flower in her hair. I noticed she had one blue eye and one green one. That somehow made me think of a cat—a cuddly kitten.

"I thought I might buy you a drink."

"Should I know who you are?"

"No. My name is Nick Saturday."

She regarded me solemnly. "That's certainly an odd name...Saturday."

"It had a wowski on the end of it once. My dad changed it in honor of payday. How about the drink?"

She smiled. "A short beer. Then I've got to dress."

I was surprised. I usually don't do very well with women. She climbed on a stool beside me. I got her the beer and she sat looking at it. She said, "You must want something. I doubt if you got my name out of the phone book."

"Does a girl named Maizie King work here?"

She thought it over, decided it was safe. "Yes. Why?"

"There were two names. Hers and yours. I heard them spoken over a telephone by a blonde in a bath towel at 1125 Weber Place."

She stiffened. "What is this? A backhanded pass, or were you just born cute?"

"It was a fact, but maybe I should have suppressed it. Sorry."

"What's your line, mister?"

I thought for a moment any decided to play it straight because I couldn't think of any other way. "I'm a private detective. I've been given the job of finding a girl you probably never heard of—a girl named Helen Burdette. I heard half a phone conversation in the apartment on Weber Place. The blonde said several things. Among them was something about a shipment with two items short. It sounded a little as though she figured you and Maizie King would become the two items to fill out the load."

TIE GIRL sat for a long time staring into her beer and I decided I'd missed. That made me feel bad, because I'd read about the clever private detectives who always turned girls into panting nymphomaniacs with one glance. They never missed. Nick Saturday—he always missed.

She said, "Maizie didn't come to work tonight." Her tone was quiet, but there was something in the tone—something a trifle breathless.

"I was hoping maybe you could help me. The blonde is tied in some way with the girl I'm looking for. Anything you've got to say would be confidential and appreciated."

Another big, silent hole, then she said, "For what it's worth to you, I was propositioned to take a trip. Well—that word *propositioned* isn't quite right. I was offered the opportunity. A two-year contract to go to a place called Timeate, or something like that."

She pronounced it Time-ate, with a long "I." Sam's version had been like in Tiny Tim, but I was willing to bet it was one and the same place.

"You turned it down?"

"Yes. I like the town I'm in." She stopped to sip her beer, the first time she'd touched it. She said, "Maizie turned it down too—and she's not at work tonight." Then she shrugged. "But there couldn't possibly be any connection."

"Probably not. Would you mind telling me who made you the offer?"

She turned her head and laid frank, but oddly bemused eyes on my face. She seemed to be counting my battle scars. She wore a tight little smile. She said, "A girl named Helen Burdette."

The barkeep came along with the scotch bottle. He filled

my glass and said, "On the house." Then he stood looking at me hopefully. I pushed a dollar bill out. He took it and strolled away, scratching his leg just above his pants pocket.

I said, "If you'll give me Maizie King's phone number I'll give her a ring and find out if she's sick. That is, if you have it."

"I have it."

"Maybe you'd rather call yourself."

"Main 4-9206."

"Thanks," I said, gratefully.

"I've got to go now."

"When are you through?"

"Four o'clock."

"I'll be right here. Same stool if it isn't filled."

"Okay." She slid off the stool. For her, it was a slide. I watched her walk away. I visualized her as being two feet high lying in an icebox. It wasn't hard to do. In her case you only had to knock off about three feet. I went out past the hatcheck girl and found a phone booth. I called Main 4-9206. There were five rings before someone answered. A female. The voice was careful. "Hello?"

"Hello:" I made it tough and brusque. "What the hell's wrong? Ain't you coming to work?"

"I—I—"

"Look—there's been too many holes in the line lately. The boss says—"

"I'm sorry. I just can't make it."

"Then don't bother from here out. Want us to mail your check?"

"No—yes—yes. Mail it."

"Okay." I slammed up the receiver.

I'D HAVE bet my poke that Maizie King hadn't been the girl on the other end of my phone call. It's not hard to trip

41

up wrongos if you're just verifying suspicions. No girl in the world would give up a job without at least a feeble attempt to hold it, even if she hated the job. It's a matter of personal pride. The party at the other end had fallen for it before she thought—fallen for it because it achieved the end she wanted: no further inquiry from Maizie King's boss.

But if she was smart she'd check back and figure the trap, so I had to hurry. Maybe it was already too late. I went back into the booth and checked the number with information. I got an address on Pine Plaza and headed for a cab.

On the way over I got qualms. Was I handling this thing right? Maybe I should call in some law, I told myself. Sure. First I'd tell them about a man I'd killed at the Hillside Sanatorium. Then, while they were still laughing, I'd spring the one about the two-foot redhead in the refrigerator. That would either rupture them or get me the nut house instead of the pen.

I leaned forward and opened the front window. "Did you ever hear of a place called Timate, or Timeate?"

The hacker leaned back. "Huh?"

"A place called Timeate—or Tim-ate."

"Uh-uh."

That was that. I closed the glass, took out my .32, and counted slugs. Four. That would get me a medium-sized rabbit at seven feet. The cab pulled up in front of the Pine Plaza. I got out and pushed a bill at the hacker. He said, "Maybe it's downstate."

"Could be. Keep the change."

There wasn't any Maizie listed on the directory. Only a Margaret. I decided the other was a nickname and checked on the door. I wouldn't have to push any buttons. I had the celluloid the phone company had put on the direction card on the Frolics night club telephone. It worked.

It worked upstairs, too, after I'd knocked three times. The

lights were on as they usually are in furnished apartments. The light goes with the rent. People don't give a damn.

It could have been any furnished apartment in any garden-variety anthill. The same phony attempt at elegance.

But that didn't interest me. I'd made it too late. That was the top news. The girl I'd talked to had been smart. She'd called back, and so the apartment was empty.

I was tired—tired as hell. I began shaking…a reaction from the dope. Then, idiotically—all of a sudden—I wondered what day it was. I hadn't asked anybody, so I didn't know. I'd been slugged early in the evening and had found my way out of the Hillside Sanatorium a little before midnight. But how many times had the earth turned?

I snapped off the light and sat down on the lounge—to let the jitters pass. I wondered if Maizie had anything in the bathroom for a headache, but didn't feel like going in to look. I wondered again whether I ought to ring in police. There was the humane obligation to Mrs. Burdette. I was willing to stake all I had that she was being held at Hillside. It was the only logical place. But there hadn't been anything very logical about this affair. Suppose I went to the police and sent them after her—and found I'd guessed wrong? The feeling of the local law toward private eyes wasn't very cordial.

All I knew for sure was that four persons had disappeared; that two-foot dolls were too human to be otherwise; that someone had wanted to keep me out of circulation. I decided to let the police handle it their way—I'd handle it mine.

The phone rang.

IT WAS Sam Kane at the Frolics Cafe. He said, "Look. I came back here hunting for you and the barkeep remembered. He rang in a little brunette babe and she gave me this number."

"What's up?"

"Something screwy. That toy factory. It's real crazy, that joint. You ought to have a look."

"Wait for me."

I went out and started looking for a cab. While I hunted, I remembered I'd had a car of my own once. I wondered where I'd left it—then remembered that too. In front of the Weber Place building. But it hadn't been there on my last visit, so somebody had taken it out of circulation. I considered having the phony Dr. Kinder hunted down as a car thief—decided it wasn't worth while. I found a cab and was dropped off in front of the Frolics. I went inside and found Sam at the bar lapping one up. He'd gotten hold of a jacket somewhere.

I asked, "What's with the toy factory?"

"If that's a toy factory I'll eat it. Everything goes in but nothing comes out."

"What goes in?"

"Well, cars mostly. Let's go over there and I'll show you—if they're still going in."

We went out and got into his hack and drove to the place. We parked across the street. It wasn't a very big building. You could have set ten of them in one block. Lights were on, but there didn't seem to be much doing.

Sam said, "I'm parked right here, casing the joint, figuring maybe I'd go over and crash in. I see three cars pull in that side entrance in a line. The door goes up—they roll in. A couple of minutes later three more cars show up—do the same thing."

"What kind?"

"New ones—light cars. No big ones. Anyhow, right on schedule, three more show up. I begin to wonder where they're all going. But I ain't seen nothing yet. You know how many cars roll into that place in an hour? Ninety-nine crates. And none came out. Where'd they all go? That joint ain't a stadium. There ain't room for that many cars in there."

I was beginning to get discouraged. New angles piling up on me from all directions. And all the while I was getting nowhere. I said, "I think you're nuts, Sam. Unless that's an entrance to some underground subway system, you've got to be nuts."

"Maybe it is—but I'm not nuts," he said stubbornly. "What are we going to do?"

"You stay here."

I got out and went across the street. The front of the building was lined with frosted glass blocks—very modernistic. A single door in the middle. There was light coming through the frosted glass, but the door had only darkness behind it. There was no bell and knocking wouldn't have done any good.

I circled the building. The only other entrance was the big gray overhead door through which—according to Sam— ninety-nine cars had recently passed. Usually those big doors have a smaller one cut into the panel so people can go in and out without lifting a ton of metal. This one had no smaller door. And again, no bell. It looked as though the Regal Toy people liked to be left alone.

I WAS GOING to get inside that place though—I knew that. But not now. I glanced at my watch. It was four-fifteen A. M. I went back to the hack and we drove to the Frolics. I hoped Jenny Davis would wait.

She was at the bar playing with a small beer when I came in. She said, "I thought you weren't coming."

"Sorry I'm late. You ready to go?"

She smiled. "I'm not going with you. I've changed my mind."

I wasn't surprised. Women had changed their minds

before so far as I was concerned. "Don't trust me, eh?"

"It's not that. Since you were here I had another visitor, Helen Burdette. I've decided to accept her offer to go to Timeate. There wasn't anything wrong at Maizie King's. Maizie decided to accept the offer too."

I knew the meaning of frustration. Nick Saturday—private eye. He went out to look for people. The people he was looking for went here and there about their business—talking to his friends—following him in and out of nightclubs and apartments. But could he lay eyes on them? Hell, no. Nick Saturday evidently wasn't equipped to find a raisin in a hot cross bun.

The barkeep came by. I ordered a double Scotch and took it in one gulp. "When are you leaving?" I asked.

"Very soon now. A young man will call for me."

"Helen Burdette didn't say where she could be reached, did she?"

Jenny gazed up at me—a little fondly, I thought, in a motherly way. "No. I mentioned you were looking for her and she seemed to know all about it. She said when she's ready to see you she'll get in touch."

At that moment a handsome young man with black curly hair and a pleasant smile came up to the bar. He stopped beside Jenny. "Miss Davis?"

"Yes."

"I'm Fred Devon. Are you ready?"

"I'll get my coat." She got off the stool and held out her hand. I took it. She said, "Good-bye and—good luck."

I said goodbye and turned away and ordered another drink. When I'd gulped it down, they were gone.

I got down on my belly and crawled across the thick carpet toward the door.

I got into the hack beside Sam. "Everything okay?" he wanted to know.

"Oh, sure—the party I'm looking for, left word for me not to worry. She'll be ready to be found any day now. When the time comes, she'll let me know."

"That's swell," Sam said. "Now you can go back and park your feet on your desk and wait."

I stifled the urge to slug him. "Drive me home. I'm going to bed."

Sam yawned. "Sure. I could use some shut-eye myself."

My place was a two-room walkup about four blocks from my office. Sam pulled up in front of it and I got out of the hack. He said, "Wait a minute."

I turned around and he dropped some small change into my hand—a quarter and two dimes. "What's this for?"

"Your change. All that's left of the fifty bucks. "I'm buying back my soul."

I handed it back. "Keep it. I always tip generously."

"Thanks—and how about a little something for the clouts I took?"

"I'll give you some business instead. Come around in the morning. We'll go hunting for my car."

"I dunno. Maybe you better hire a detective."

He got away before I could swing on him.

I went in and climbed the two flights to my crow's nest. All I wanted was a bed. Maybe after a few hour's sleep things would look better. Hell—everybody is entitled to a little sleep once in a while. Even the world's stupidest detective.

But sleep wasn't in the cards. My bed was in use. A blonde was sitting on it.

CHAPTER FIVE

I SAID, "Miss Keating, I believe." She was cool as an icicle in an electric blue dress above a nice expanse of nylon hose. The dress was exquisitely filled, and it occurred to me that we had a secret between us. We both knew what filled it. "How did you know my name? I don't remember mentioning it?"

"It was on the door to your apartment. I spotted it. Probably no one else would have, but you see...I'm a detective."

"That's right—I forgot."

I sat down in my only chair, facing her. "It was nice of you to drop in."

"Wasn't it? I've been waiting for two hours."

"It must be important."

"It is. I was sent around to straighten you out."

"Who sent you?"

"Let's call it the syndicate. That's a good name and it covers almost anything."

"So they think I need straightening out?"

She eyed me critically. "What do you think?"

"Maybe you've got something. Do you do it on an anvil?"

"You've been running around having a lot of fun and you think you've uncovered a lot of dastardly deeds. As a matter of fact, everything you found is quite in order."

I couldn't think of a comeback and she went on: "Let's start at the beginning. You went out hunting for Helen Burdette and went, illegally, into her mother's apartment. We could have you arrested for that."

"We weren't talking about me."

"But we wouldn't bother making a complaint. You found Mrs. Burdette in shock and decided sinister agencies were at work. The truth of the matter was that both Mrs. Burdette and Helen had just returned from Time Eight and had gotten fouled up. Nothing serious—nothing serious at all."

The way she pronounced it, *Time Eight*, left no doubt about how it was spelled. I said, "You're going a little too fast. First, where is Time Eight? Second, how do you get back and forth?"

This gave her pause. "I can't tell you that yet. It's a little too complicated. We'll just go on the supposition that Time Eight is a place you can get fouled up coming back from. Okay?"

"If you say so."

Another pause. "Do you like my legs?"

"What if I said no?"

"I'd call you a liar. Right now please pay attention to what I'm saying. You can look at them later."

I SHOULD have gotten mad, but I was too tired—and curious. My eyes had been on her legs because my eyes were heavy and her legs were closer to the floor than her face.

She said, "The doll had nothing to do with it. It just happened to be there."

"The guy that conked me just happened to be there too, I suppose?"

"He was under orders to stay with the Burdettes until help arrived. You barged in. He felt the situation was none of your business. He slugged you."

"Sounds reasonable."

"It was reasonable. Then, while he came downstairs for orders, you woke up and called a doctor. From there on out we had to proceed as best we could. We intercepted Dr.

Kinder—"

"What did you do with him?"

"Never mind—nothing sinister. Then we moved in and took Mrs. Burdette away."

"And a two-foot, living doll you put—"

She brushed it aside impatiently. "That was Helen Burdette. She hadn't orientated."

"I don't know what that means, but what I saw in your refrigerator looked dead to me."

The impatience persisted. "Helen can't die. It's an impossibility. But will you stop interrupting? I don't want to stay here all night."

"Go ahead."

"After we got Mrs. Burdette out, we were willing to call it quits—to let you alone. But no—you wouldn't have it that way. You had to come back and stick your big face into it again."

"So you slugged me again."

"What did you expect? We had no plan for taking care of you. We just put you out of circulation until we could originate a plan. But you went hog wild. You killed Cooper—"

"What did you expect?" I mimicked. "I kind of had the idea I might be fighting for my life."

"That's why we're not holding it against you. He was a nice boy and you'll have to carry it on your conscience. Luckily Tate came through all right. And Gleason got over his headache."

"That's too bad."

"Don't be so belligerent. When you walked out of the Sanatorium we were willing to call it quits again. We thought maybe you'd had enough. But not our bully-boy. Back you came. So that's why I'm here."

She crossed her legs and tapped one neat foot on the

floor. "Now—are all your questions answered?"

"You haven't even started."

"Let me put it another way. Would you like to be a rich man?"

"Not necessarily."

I was trying her patience, but she was holding on. "Do you see anything else around that you'd like?"

"Look, for what I lack in brilliance I make up in stubbornness. I started out to find Helen Burdette for a certain party. I'll keep on hunting until he tells me to stop."

That seemed to remind her of something. She reached down and lifted her skirt until it cleared the top of her stocking. Inside the stocking was tucked a roll of bills. She took them out and handed them to me. "There's your money. Your pants are out at the sanatorium."

I took the dough and shoved it into my pocket. "Thanks. I'll pick up the pants as soon as these need pressing."

We sat there for a few moments measuring each other with scant cordiality. Then I said, "By the way, what do you people do with dead bodies? Throw them in the ashcan?"

"You mean Cooper? We took him back to Time Eight."

"There's another thing I'm going to find out about if it will help me locate Helen Burdette. A lot of questions have got to be answered."

Winona Keating got to her feet. "All right. I'll tell her. I'll go back and report that you're incorruptible, and we'll be in touch with you." She got to her feet and stood looking down at me. "Incorruptible, but not bulletproof."

She went to the door, opened it, and turned again. "So long. And don't call us. We'll call you."

She went out.

I went to bed.

I WOKE up at three that afternoon. I got up and made

coffee and smoked a cigarette. I was going to have to report to Mike Conlin, but what was I going to report? Almost anything I told him would be grounds for putting me away in a crazy coop. But he was my client, and private eyes are supposed to report to their clients at fairly reasonable intervals.

I shaved and went over to report. I found Mike fixing a safety valve on the furnace. He gave me a grin and wiped the grease off his hands. "How's it coming? Long time no see."

"Nothing to tell you about, except that I haven't found your girl yet."

He had no reply. We walked up the ramp between two hot-water tanks into his apartment. There was a pot of coffee on the stove. He got a pair of cups and we sat down. Mike studied me. "You don't look so good. Tough going?"

"No worse than you'd expect."

He put down his cup. "Helen came to see me last night."

I was past being embarrassed. In fact, I'd half expected something like that. "I guess that makes a monkey out of me."

"I can't see it that way. Maybe you didn't catch up with her, but I don't think she'd have come here if you hadn't been on the trail."

"Did you ask her any questions?"

"Like which?"

"Like where she'd been? Like what happened to her mother? Like what the hell's been going on?"

"I showed an interest, but I didn't press. What about her mother?"

"She wasn't in the County."

"Helen took her away?"

"Somebody took her away."

"Helen wasn't worried. She didn't even mention her mother, so I guess everything is all right."

"She didn't tell you where she'd been?"

"Traveling," she said. "Laughed off the whole thing."

Something had been bothering me ever since Winona Keating told me that both Helen and her mother had returned from this place called Time Eight. Now I brought it up. "I wonder how the word got around that Helen was missing—how it got into the paper."

Mike said, "As it matter of fact, it was my fault. Indirectly. I lied to you when I implied that seeing the item brought Helen back to my mind. I'd been thinking about her a lot. I called her and found she'd left her old place without leaving a forwarding address. I asked a newspaperman—a friend of mine—to check on it. Those guys are supposed to have connections. He turned up the fact that she was missing and published the item."

"I see. That explains a point."

"What point?"

"An unimportant one."

Mike didn't press it. He stared vaguely at his cigarette. "Helen was quite interested in you. She asked a lot of questions. Who you were—where you came from."

"What did you tell her?"

"Anything I could. I didn't see any harm in it."

"There was no harm. I'm not important enough to clam up on." I snubbed out my cigarette. "Well, I guess you won't be needing my services any more.

He thought that over. "I think you'd better keep at it a little while longer. Helen was worried about something. I think she may be in some kind of trouble. Maybe you can help her."

"How can I help her when I can't even find her? Everybody in town's seen her during the last twenty-four hours except me. You're wasting your money."

He grinned. But it was a bleak grin. He wasn't very

happy. "Maybe she'll find you if she needs you. Anyhow, keep at it. Let me know if anything develops."

I wasn't completely stupid. I said, "You just don't want to let go completely, do you? It would be too final."

"That's about it. You're operating for me by proxy." He got to his steel feet. "I've got to get back to work. Keep in touch."

I told him I would, and went up to my office. I wasn't in any hurry to start after Helen Burdette. I figured Winona Keating hadn't been fooling when she'd said they'd get in touch with me. Everything indicated I was too hot to let alone—from their point of view, of course.

One way or another, though, I knew I had to get back at it. There were too many unanswered questions. I never liked questions without answers. I was getting awfully interested in a place called Time Eight, not to mention a few minor conundrums relative to two-foot human dolls and ninety-nine cars rolling into the Regal Toy Company. I thought it over and decided there was no time like the present. I went out and caught a cab and headed west.

CHAPTER SIX

I STOOD across the street from the alleged toy factory trying to figure out if there was anything unusual about it. I decided there wasn't. I crossed the street and went in the front door. I found a small, luxurious waiting room with a pretty girl sitting beside a PBX board and behind a desk. The walls were restful green, the chairs luxurious. A man with a briefcase—probably a salesman—was nodding in one of the chairs.

I went to the reception desk and said, "I want to see Winona Keating."

The girl seemed puzzled. She studied me vaguely and then

opened a directory book at her elbow. "I'm sorry, we have no Winona Keating with us. Are you sure you have the name right?"

"How about Helen Burdette?"

She didn't have to look in the book. "No one by that name, either."

I said, "Look, honey—I'm tired of the runaround. I've decided to find out what I want to know, or make a fool out of myself. I want to see either or both of the ladies I've named. If I don't see them pretty quick, I'll get the police and come back and we'll check your records together. Is that clear?"

The girl seemed genuinely distressed. She stared at me as though wondering whether or not it would be worth while to appeal to my common sense. She decided not, got up from her chair and said, "Pardon me for a moment—please." She went out through a rear door.

I stood by the desk waiting. I didn't know quite what to do so I did nothing, although I realized I'd probably flubbed it again. The girl had no doubt gone to warn my quarry. Even now they were probably kiting it out the back door.

The salesman had perked up. He regarded me with interest for a moment or two, then picked up his briefcase and put it across his knees as though he figured I had designs on it.

The girl came back. She said, "Take him to Transfer Three." She wasn't speaking to me. She was talking to the man with the briefcase.

He had a gun in his hand now. He got up and came up close and put the gun into my back. He said, "Okay, buster. No trouble now. Let's go." As he spoke, he expertly frisked me and lifted the .32 from my hip pocket. He grinned at it. "My—aren't we tough? Come on. Move."

We went through the rear door into a hall running at right

angles. He nudged me and I turned left. We walked single file for perhaps fifty feet. Then I stopped suddenly, waited a split second, and brought my elbow up sharply into the pit of the man's stomach.

He grunted in pain, doubled over, and I had my hand on his gun wrist. I twisted it back and found he'd be pretty easy to handle.

But he yelled.

Before I could put him out of commission, he let out a honey of a yelp—twice repeated—that must have carried all over the building.

THINGS BEGAN happening fast then. Three doors opened onto the hall and three huskies appeared—so quickly it seemed they must have been crouching behind the doors waiting for the yell.

I was blocked off at both ends. The closest door—my only possible exit—was about ten feet away. I dived for it, not waiting to pick up the fallen gun. They were coming so fast I wouldn't have had time anyhow.

I went through the doorway—fast—and fell down a flight of stairs. A landing stopped me. By the time I was on my feet my lead pursuer was there, reaching for me. I swung. He had a glass chin.

The stairs began spiraling from that first landing. I kited downward. No one chased me. The remaining two bully boys stopped up above and began yelling. I speeded up, trying to reach bottom before a reception committee formed down there.

I couldn't see much from where I was—not that it wasn't there to be seen. I was just spinning around too fast. What I did see appeared to be a huge storehouse, and it was certainly full of a number of things. Bright new automobiles, shiny chrome bathroom fixtures, refrigerators, wooden crates, steel crates, paper crates, modernistic furniture, antique furniture, overstuffed furniture. But no toys that I could see.

A single character was waiting at the foot of the staircase to dispute my passage. I won the dispute with a kick in the stomach and a straight right and went on my way. I ran along the wall until I could see that I'd end up in a blind alley. Fortunately, I found another door before this happened, went through it, and ran down another corridor. This formed a T at the far end. I turned left and went through a door at the end of the cross-corridor. Once beyond it I stopped dead in my tracks—pursuit forgotten—my danger forgotten—everything forgotten—washed from my mind by the sight before me.

I stood in a stainless steel room. Near one wall of this room was a vat of shining metal—a tub in which fluid bubbled and boiled. The fluid had all the appearance of molten metal, but I didn't study it too closely. There were other things of greater interest.

Hanging over the vat from two metal arms was the body of a naked girl. She appeared to be unconscious, possibly from the fumes rising from the vat.

And as I watched, she grew smaller—shrank before my eyes, into a two-foot, lovely, redheaded doll.

The wall beyond the vat was made up, mainly, of a heavy glass panel. Beyond this, a man in a white coat manipulated two steel arms that obviously controlled the ones from which the girl was suspended. He worked entirely with his thumbs and a finger of each hand, and his concentration was such that he did not appear to even see me.

The door behind me opened. I started to turn, but my reflexes were bad. I'd been paying too much attention to unimportant things—things like a vat of lava, a shrinking girl, a man with a tense, perspiring face.

When the sap came down on my head it was like old

times.

I CAME TO—but not completely. It was, rather, like entering a dream state. I was partially aware of what was going on, but could do nothing about it. It seemed that I too was hanging in space, supported by two rods. There was something resembling great heat, but not entirely the same. This heat seemed of a penetrating variety that worked more on the nerves than on the flesh. I felt as though I'd been skewered on a million hot wires.

Then there was a flame of color piercing my eyelids—all the colors of the spectrum. This lasted for approximately seventeen centuries, during which time I tried to regain my senses and achieve muscular control. I did neither.

Now I was lifted from the hooks and carried lightly—as though by giants. After a while they laid me down. I heard retreating footsteps—a door closing—a sound as of many bolts slipping into place.

I managed to open my eyes.

I lay on a table in a small, square room of bright metal. The table had a foam-rubber mattress of some sort and was not uncomfortable. I was somehow reminded of the steam room of a Turkish bath. I lifted my head and shoulders from the table.

Then the strength went out of me as invisible bolts of power hit me hard—sapped my strength—burrowed into my flesh, my bones—drained me.

I opened my eyes. The room was getting smaller—smaller—closing in on me. Then a thousand rainbows split into atoms and I dropped out of the parade.

I WAS LYING on a lounge in a strange room. It was huge, luxurious, with sunlight blazing in high windows. I blinked at the unaccustomed light and got to my feet. From the windows came sounds of activity beyond.

I wondered whether this was reality or a dream. If a dream it had none of the illusionary qualities of such. I felt completely alive, entirely alert. And if my preceding experience had been reality, it had left no ill effects. I walked to a window and looked out.

Below was a broad, clean avenue between buildings of ancient Greek and Roman architecture. A marble boulevard, shining in the sun. A stunning conglomeration of vehicles rolled along the thoroughfare. Roman chariots drawn by spirited horses; automobiles of modern design; strange conveyances of a futuristic nature, stemming obviously from the automobiles of today, yet far ahead in beauty and efficiency.

And the people. It seemed they couldn't make up their minds what they wanted to be. There were Roman togas and flowing Greek robes in evidence. Powdered and bewigged dandies and ladies from the courts of the French kings rubbed elbows with modern business suits, sports togs, and clothing resembling nothing I'd ever seen. My mind hunted a comparison and found it in thoughts of a huge movie set.

I laughed in the grip of sudden of light-headedness. Footsteps sounded. I turned.

A girl entered the room. She wore brief clothing of shining, metallic cloth. Her hair was the yellow of flowing gold and was done in a twisting, sinuous hairdo.

She carried a tray of fruit, some of it familiar. Bananas, oranges, apples. And some of strange color and shape I couldn't classify.

The girl smiled. "For your inner comfort," she said.

I ignored the tray. "What place is this?"

"Time Eight, of course."

"What is Time Eight?"

She seemed bewildered. "Why—it is this city, this

country, this world. Time Eight."

"How did I get here?"

"Through the transfer, I suppose. How else?"

"I don't understand. What is the transfer?"

This confused her even more. "You mean you don't know? Weren't you asked to come here?"

There was a penetrating sound from overhead. I turned and looked out the window to see a fleet of planes fly across the sky. But here again was strangeness. Sleek and rocket-like in design, they marked a new era in air travel so far as I was concerned.

"No, I wasn't asked to come here. I don't know where *here* is."

The girl evidently wanted to help, but didn't know how to go about it. She finally indicated the fruit bowl. "Maybe something to eat would build up your strength," she said.

"I don't need my strength built up," I snapped. "I want to see whoever's in charge of this casting bureau."

"Casting bureau?"

"Never mind. Who's your boss?"

AT THIS moment a panel opened in the wall. A girl stepped through. The panel closed. The girl said, "Run along, Theresa," without looking at the girl. The latter ducked her head in quick deference, as though glad to quit the presence of a goof who didn't know what transfer meant.

The girl who had come out of the woodwork wore the same metal-cloth costume as the fruit bearer. She was prettier, though, and obviously of much higher caliber. She said, "Nick Saturday. At last we meet."

I watched the light throw gleaming bands off her red hair. I said, "We met before. In a refrigerator. You've grown up since. You *are* Helen Burdette, *aren't* you?

She laughed. "Yes. Won't you sit down? I'm sure you'd

like some questions answered. We might as well be comfortable." She sat down on the lounge.

I stood where I was. "Why was I brought here?"

"You made known a desire to find me. Certain people assisted you."

"That's not much of an answer."

She tapped a fingernail against a white tooth, then said: "Suppose you start with more pertinent questions. We'll work back to your first one."

"All right. What do you intend to do with me?"

"That depends on you."

"Where is this place—this Time Eight? What is it?"

"It's a time cycle, almost the same as the one you came from—Time Two. You see, creation is pretty much a matter of various rates of vibration occupying the same space. Perhaps you can visualize it better by imagining there are numerous worlds functioning concurrently, each partially interlocked with the others."

I opened my mouth for another question, but she brushed it aside. "Let me tell you what you want to know," she said. "If I don't make it clear, you can ask questions later."

"Okay."

"This world you're in now is called Time Eight, even by it's own inhabitants. It's like Time Two, the one from which you came, in most respects. It is a so-called *parasite* time band, however, while your Time Two is a productive band.

"This means that we have nothing here but the natural facilities for existence. We draw on other productive time bands for everything we have. The people of Time Eight are entirely aware of this. Therefore they are far ahead of the people of the productive bands so far as knowledge goes. They are, I believe, more civilized and further advanced.

"As a matter of fact, our world population is made up entirely of immigrants. They were invited here to live. They come of their own choice."

She stopped for breath.

I said, "Let's get a little more specific. Just who are you?"

HELEN BURDETTE smiled. "Up to two years ago I was just what I appeared to be—an ordinary girl working at an ordinary job in your ordinary world. Then I was contacted by the leaders of Time Eight and offered an important job in procurement. You see, the people here, under our advanced system, draw on all the productive bands for what they want. My job is to see that orders drawn on Time Two are filled. The Regal Toy Company is one of our transfer points. The apartments in the Weber Place building are for my mother, myself, and members of my organization."

"A bunch of gangsters—"

She refused to ruffle. "Not at all. But this business requires complete secrecy. Our approach to it must be practical. It functions with extreme efficiency, but at times there is a specialized situation—such as occurred when you began functioning as a private eye."

I wondered if there was mockery in the tone. "And the Hillside Sanatorium?"

"We are continually extending invitations to people of Time Two, as well as other worlds. Just now we need women in Time Eight. Many of those we invite, who agree to come, are not physically up to the ordeal of transfer. Hillside is one of the places where we build up their physical stamina."

"You mean the transfer is dangerous?"

"Very."

"How many times have you gone back and forth?"

"I've lost count."

My resentment was somewhat dulled by the courage represented here. "You must love death, baby, to court it so often. Why do you do it?"

She shrugged. "What is it called in Time Two? Patriotism—love of country? It would be hard for you to understand us here in Time Eight. We have an entirely different level of thinking. Some of our philosophies would amaze you. But there is still loyalty."

My mind snapped back to practicalities. "What's the truth about the human dolls? I found you lying in the icebox. And that was you suspended over the vat, wasn't it?"

"Yes." Her eyes were on me with an almost amused light. "How tall do you think you are, Nick Saturday?"

"Six feet two."

"No. Height, my friend, is a matter of comparison. You were six feet-two in Time Two, and it seems to you that you haven't changed, but you have. There is a lessened molecular comparison between the two worlds. That makes Time Eight much smaller. Thus, all things, human and otherwise, have to be reduced before transfer. In Time Eight—as you are at this moment—you would fit easily into a refrigerator." She indicated the fruit bowl. "That orange would be as small as a large marble. In comparison, this is a doll-sized world."

"That's why ninety-nine cars could roll into the toy factory?"

"Yes. We have an automatic reducing unit for all inanimate objects. They are transferred quickly."

"Do you have a reducing and transfer unit on Weber Place?"

"No. My presence there in reduced form was due to an error—an emergency that is of no great importance to you. It also was unfortunate in that it started you out on the sequence of events that ended in Cooper's death."

"The man I killed?"

"We are not holding it against you. You were, to a great extent, justified. The methods used by our organization there were—well, somewhat drastic, but that was because of inexperienced personnel who were panicked."

I ASKED, "How is your mother?" and the words sounded stilted—somehow out of place—too personal.

"Very well, thank you. She returned to Time Eight with me. She will stay here."

"That gets us back to my original question. What happens to me?"

There had been a tone of light carelessness, almost mockery, in her explanations. Now she sobered. "I don't quite know. There are several factors involved. Your case may require a major rearrangement in our system."

"Why?"

"Because you are not here after the regular manner of entry. You'd be surprised how carefully our prospective immigrants are approached, scrutinized, studied. It is by far the most exhaustive phase of our work."

"Maybe I'd like to stay for good. That would simplify things, wouldn't it?"

"Only partially. Your inclinations are only a phase of it. Perhaps you aren't emotionally and mentally fitted for this world. Perhaps you don't belong here."

"You mean everyone here belongs, beyond any doubt?"

"Oh, yes." She was watching me narrowly. "Suppose you rest now. The transfer is deceptively weakening. Tomorrow you can go before the examining board. That is, if you would care to look into the possibilities of staying."

"I think I'd like to look into them."

"Very well." She got up and moved toward the panel. It opened, seemingly having a mind of its own. "I'll come for you tomorrow. If you want anything, just ring."

CHAPTER SEVEN

THE EXAMINING board was certainly composed of a motley crew. There were two Romans right out of Caesar's cabinet. A Greek who could have palled around with Plato. An Englishman dressed like Lord Nelson. A couple of Buck Rogers' lieutenants. They asked a lot of questions. Such as:

"Mr. Saturday…if you found two dogs injured in the road—one a huge St. Bernard, and one a small Spaniel—which would you aid first?"

"I don't know. The one most badly hurt, I guess."

"If you could be either the president of the United States, or the king of ancient Egypt, which would you be?"

"Neither job appeals to me very much."

"Do you consider appetizing food as one of life's major luxuries?"

"I—I guess so."

"What was the date of the Battle of Tours?"

"I don't know."

"Emil Coue, a Frenchman, originated a phrase: 'Every day, in every way, I'm getting better and better.' Do you believe it had any therapeutic value?"

"No."

"If you had a splitting headache and were handed an unmarked bottle of white pills by a friend, would you swallow one without question?"

"I—I think so. Yes—I would."

"Why do you want to live in Time Eight, Mr. Saturday?"

"It appears to be an ideal world."

"Do you think the climate of Earth has changed any in the

last one hundred years?"

"No."

"Do you believe in God?"

"Yes."

"Do you expect to go to hell for killing Revlon Cooper?"

"I don't know."

More and more of the same. One hour. Two hours. Three hours, until I got the idea they were trying to ruffle me. I refused to ruffle. I could stand it if they could.

Finally the questions came to an end. The board got up and filed from the room. The clerk, an Oriental wearing sandals and a brightly-colored Hawaiian breechclout, said, "You may return to your quarters, Mr. Saturday. You will be made aware of the board's decision."

I went back to my room and looked out the window. I paced the floor. The girl brought dinner but I couldn't eat any. I wished Helen Burdette would pay me a visit.

The more I thought of living in Time Eight, the better I liked it. It would be a little like being born again. Learning of a new world—a new life. I found myself waiting with growing impatience.

But no one came to tell me of the board's decision. Finally, I drifted off to sleep.

I WAS LYING on the cramped I lounge in my office. My mouth tasted like the bottom of a cage tenanted by a very messy bird. If what I had was not a hangover, it would do until I could acquire one. I got up and went to the wash basin and looked in the mirror. It was me all right—with a four-day growth of beard, bloodshot eyes and a sense of bewilderment.

I went through the motions of shaving, then sat down behind my desk and tried to catch up with myself. Gradually it all came back. But how could it be classified? A bad dream? No dream could be that wild. I went clear back to the beginning—when Mike Conlin had walked into my office. At the moment I honestly decided it had all been a dream.

But there was a way to check on it. I went down and knocked on Mike's door. There was no answer. I opened the door and went inside. Mike wasn't there. The rooms were very quiet. There was a feeling of desertion about them. The bedding gone. Only a bare mattress on the springs. Dust everywhere. Mike had been neat. I went down into the boiler room.

A wizened little man in greasy overalls looked up from a pipe he was working on. I had never seen him before. I said. "Where's Mike Conlin?"

He cupped his ear and said, "Eh?"

"Mike Conlin. Mike Conlin—the man that owns this building."

"Oh, him. He died quite a spell back." The man went into conference with his recollection. "About six months ago it was—maybe seven."

"Dead? What the hell you talking about?"

"You asked me, mister. I told you. Who are you, anyway?" Maybe the little guy had a right to be belligerent, but I wasn't paying any attention. He peered at me closely. "What's your name, mister? I ain't seen you around."

I said, "Look—what happened to Nick Saturday, the private investigator who had offices in this building?"

The janitor scratched his head. "Saturday—Saturday. Oh, yeah. I remember. The guy disappeared. Guess he took a powder. The police were around asking about him."

"How come his office is still there?"

"Since Mr. Conlin died the place has been tied up. Can't rent nothing. Can't move until the courts get through with it. I dunno."

He only now realized he had been cross-examined. He

resented it. "Look here, mister. Who the hell—"

I said, "Thanks," and went out into the street. I went to the corner and bought a newspaper. I looked at the date and figured. Eight months—more—almost nine. I stood there for a long time. Then I began walking.

I WALKED for twenty minutes before I had sense enough to hail a cab. I got in and said, "Hillside Sanatorium." The hacker drove about two blocks, then stopped and turned around to look at me. He said, "Hey, bud, it's none of my business. I could collect a fare but—that hospital burned down over a month ago. Big fire. You from out of town?"

I said, "Yeah, I'm from out of town. Take me to the Regal Toy Company."

"You know the address?"

I thought hard and gave him the address.

The Regal Toy Company was still there. And the reception room hadn't changed except that the phony salesman with the briefcase was missing. I asked the girl for Helen Burdette. She tapped her teeth with a pencil and told me Miss Burdette was out of town. I asked for Winona Keating.

The girl talked over an intercom and, a few minutes later, I walked into an office and looked at a blonde girl across a big desk. I asked, "Just what is your job here?"

I tried to analyze her look. Surprise, of course, and maybe some fear, but no resentment. She said, "I am Miss Burdette's assistant."

I don't think she recognized me. We looked at each other for a long minute. Then she said, "Is there something I can do for you?"

I said, "You've already done it."

"I don't understand."

"I just wanted to find something, or somebody, to prove

that it all wasn't a dream. I know now. I'll be seeing you."

I walked out mad as a hatter. I don't know why anger was my reaction to it all. I just had an overwhelming feeling of having been pushed around too much. I had a case for the cops. A lot of it was pretty dim in my mind, but I knew this rat's nest had to be cleaned out.

TWENTY MINUTES later I came back with some law. Two uniformed men and a detective. I didn't even remember their names two minutes after I heard them. They were only law to me. Blank faces.

The detective pulled the door open and said, "I hope you know what you're doing."

I said, "At the very least you're going to have a case of exporting without a license."

"That's Federal."

"But you'll enjoy turning it up. And you're going to turn some other things up. I don't know what you'll call them."

We asked for Winona Keating. We waited. Helen Burdette came through the door.

I said, "I thought you were out of town."

She stared in wonder. "I don't understand."

"Skip it."

The detective said, "Madam, we have no legal rights here—at the moment—but I wonder if you'd object to our going through your factory?"

"Not at all," Helen Burdette replied. "This way."

She started off toward the wrong door. I said, "No—we'll go this way," and headed for the route I'd previously taken. The law followed me. I said. "Through this hall. There's a stairway. All the loot is in the basement."

We found the stairs—and the basement. But the loot wasn't there. Nothing but a factory. Long assembly lines with girls in neat rows turning out things for kiddies. Helen

Burdette said. "This is our rush season. We will run two shifts for several months. Were there some questions?"

It seemed that the Regal Toy Company made toys. At least there was no use telling the law any different. The detective looked at me as he said, "What have you got to say?"

I told him I didn't have anything to say. He scowled. "I ought to have you taken in and examined. Watch your step, or that's you're going to land—in psycho."

I didn't say anything. I was thinking. I was thinking he was right. I'd gone off my rocker. I was in bad shape. I said, "Sorry," and shuffled toward the stairs. We went back to the reception room. The detective apologized to Helen Burdette. Then the three of them headed for the door. I turned to follow them.

Helen Burdette stepped close to me. "I'm sorry," she said, in a low voice. "The board decided against you."

I straightened lip and grinned. I said. "That's okay, baby. That's just fine."

I went out into the street. The police car was pulling away. I called a cab and gave the hacker a certain street corner. As we crossed town, I wondered if Sam Kane was still on the job. I had a feeling he was.

THE END

WELCOME TO FRUYLING'S WORLD

Fruyling's world was tremendously rich in precious metals. The kinds of metals that kept the Terran Confederation going. The planet's output was a vital link to a galaxy-wide civilization.

But the men of Fruyling's World were living on borrowed time. They knew that slavery was outlawed throughout the Confederation. Unfortunately for them, only the slave labor of the reptilian natives could produce the precious metals the Confederation needed! It was a real problem, and as the first hints of the truth about Fruyling's World emerged, the tension became unbearable—to be resolved only in a shattering climax.

Laurence Janifer's "Slave Planet" is a fast-paced, thought-provoking story you'll long remember.

CAST OF CHARACTERS

DR. ANNA HAENLINGER
Icy, reserved, the architect of the system that kept men on top and aliens enslaved.

JOHNNY DODD
He had everything a man could want on Fruyling's World— except the freedom from the horror of being there.

NORMA FREDERICKS
Warm and human, she was Dodd's one hope for salvation.

CADNAN
He did what he was told…until the Masters told him to die!

MARVOR
The first to have an independent idea—an idea that was dangerous and deadly.

DARA
Green and reptilian, but beautiful enough to inspire Cadnan to the slave world's worst crime.

SLAVE PLANET

By
LAURENCE M. JANIFER

ARMCHAIR FICTION
PO Box 4369, Medford, Oregon 97504

For more information about Armchair Books and products, visit our website at...

www.armchairfiction.com

Or email us at...

armchairfiction@yahoo.com

PART ONE

FOREWORD

"On Saturday, July 30, Dr. Johnson and I took a sculler at the Temple-stairs, and set out for Greenwich. I asked him if he really thought a knowledge of the Greek and Latin languages an essential requisite to a good education. JOHNSON: 'Most certainly, Sir; for those who know them have a very great advantage over those who do not. Nay, Sir, it is wonderful what a difference learning makes upon people even in the common intercourse of life, which does not appear to be much connected with it.' 'And yet, (said I) people go through the world very well, and carry on the business of life to good advantage, without learning.' JOHNSON: 'Why, Sir, that may be true in cases where learning cannot possibly be of any use; for instance, this boy rows us as well without learning, as if he could sing the song of Orpheus to the Argonauts, who were the first sailors.' He then called to the boy, 'What would you give my lad, to know about the Argonauts?' 'Sir, (said the boy) I would give what I have.' Johnson was much pleased with his answer, and we gave him a double fare. Dr. Johnson then turning to me, 'Sir, (said he) a desire of knowledge is the natural feeling of mankind; and every human being, whose mind is not debauched, will be willing to give all that he has, to get knowledge.' "

—James Boswell,
The Life of Samuel Johnson, L. L. D.

"It has become a common catchword that slavery is the product of an agricultural society and cannot exist in the contemporary, mechanized world. Like so many catchwords, this one is recognizable as nonsense as soon as it is closely examined. Given that the upkeep of the slaves is less than the price of full automation (and *its* upkeep), I do not think we shall prove ourselves morally so very superior to our grandfathers."

—H. D. Abel,

Essays in History and Causation.

CHAPTER ONE

"I WOULD not repeat myself if it were not for the urgency of this matter." Dr. Haenlingen's voice hardly echoed in the square small room. She stood staring out at the forests below, the coiling gray-green trees, the plants and rough growth. A small woman whose carriage was always, publicly, stiff and erect, whose iron-gray eyes seemed as solid as ice, she might years before have trained her voice to sound improbably flat and formal. Now the formality was dissolving in anger. "As you know, the mass of citizens throughout the Confederation are a potential source of explosive difficulty, and our only safety against such an explosion lies in complete and continuing silence." Abruptly, she turned away from the window. "Have you got that, Norma?"

Norma Fredericks nodded, her trace poised over the waiting pad. "Yes, Dr. Haenlingen. Of course."

Dr. Haenlingen's laugh was a dry rustle. "Good Lord, girl," she said. "Are you afraid of me, too?"

Norma shook her head instantly, then stopped and almost smiled. "I suppose I am, Doctor," she said. "I don't quite know why—"

"Authority figure, parent-surrogate, phi factor—there's no mystery about the why, Norma. If you're content with jargon, and we know all the jargon, don't we?" Now instead of a laugh it was a smile, surprisingly warm but very brief. "We ought to, after all, we ladle it out often enough."

Norma said, "There's certainly no real reason for fear. I don't want you to think—"

"I don't think," Dr. Haenlingen said. "I never think. I reason when I must, react when I can." She paused. "Sometimes, Norma, it strikes me that the Psychological Division hasn't really kept track of its own occupational syndromes."

"Yes?" Norma waited, a study in polite attention. The trace fell slowly in her hand to the pad on her knees and rested there.

"I ask you if you're afraid of me and I get the beginnings of a self-analysis," Dr. Haenlingen said. She walked three steps to the desk and sat down behind it, her hands clasped on the surface, her eyes staring at the younger woman. "If I'd let you go on I suppose you could have given me a yard and a half of assorted psychiatric jargon, complete with suggestions for a change in your pattern."

"I only—"

"You only reacted the way a good Psychological Division worker is supposed to react, I imagine." The eyes closed for a second, opened again. "You know, Norma, I could have dictated this to a tape and had it sent out automatically. Did you stop to think why I wanted to talk it out to you?"

"It's a message to the Confederation," Norma said slowly. "I suppose it's important, and you wanted—"

"Importance demands accuracy," Dr. Haenlingen broke in. "Do you think you can be more accurate than a tape record?"

A second of silence went by. "I don't know, then," Norma said at last.

"I wanted reaction," Dr. Haenlingen said. "I wanted somebody's reaction. But I can't get yours. As far as I can see you're the white hope of the Psychological Division—but even you are afraid of me, even you are masking any reaction you might have for fear the terrifying Dr. Anna Haenlingen won't like it." She paused. "Good Lord, girl, I've got to know if I'm getting through!"

Norma took a deep breath. "I'm sorry," she said at last. "I'll try to give you what you want—"

"There you go again." Dr. Haenlingen shoved back her chair and stood up, marched to the window and stared out at the forest again. Below, the vegetation glowed in the daylight. She shook her head slowly. "How can you give me what I want when I don't know what I want? I need to know what you think, how you react. I'm not going to bite your head off if you do something wrong. There's nothing wrong that you *can* do. Except not react at all."

"I'm sorry," Norma said again.

Dr. Haenlingen's shoulders moved, up and down. It might have been a sigh. "Of course you are," she said in a gentler voice. "I'm sorry, too. It's just that matters aren't getting any better—and one false move could crack us wide open."

"I know," Norma said. "You'd think people would understand—"

"People," Dr. Haenlingen said, "understand very little. That's what we're here for, Norma, to make them understand a little more. To make them understand, in fact, what we want them to understand."

"The truth," Norma said.

"Of course," Dr. Haenlingen said, almost absently. "The truth."

This time there was a longer pause.

"Shall we get on with it, then?" Dr. Haenlingen said.

"I'm ready," Norma said. " 'Complete and continuing silence.' "

Dr. Haenlingen paused. "What? Oh...it should be perfectly obvious that the average Confederation citizen, regardless of his training or information, would not understand the project under development here no matter how carefully it was explained to him. The very concepts of freedom, justice, equality under the law, which form the cornerstone of Confederation law and, more importantly, Confederation societal patterns, will prevent him from judging with any real degree of objectivity our actions on Fruyling's World, or our motives."

"Actions," Norma muttered. "Motives." The trace flew busily over the pad, leaving its shorthand trail.

"It was agreed in the original formation of our project here that silence and secrecy were essential to the project's continuance. Now, in the third generation of that project, the wall of silence has been breached and I have received repeated reports of rumors regarding our relationship with the natives. The very fact that such rumors exist is indication enough that an explosive situation is developing. It is possible for the Confederation to be forced to the wall on this issue, and this issue alone. I cannot emphasize too strongly the fact that such a possibility exists. Therefore—"

"Doctor," Norma said.

The dictation stopped. Dr. Haenlinger turned slowly. "Yes?"

"You wanted reactions, didn't you?" Norma said.

"Well?" The word was not unfriendly.

Norma hesitated for a second. Then she burst out: "But they're so far away! I mean—there isn't any reason why they should really care. They're busy with their own lives, and I don't really see why whatever's done here should occupy them—"

"Because you're not seeing them," Dr. Haenlingen said. "Because you're thinking of the Confederation, not the people who compose the Confederation, all of the people on Mars, and Venus, the moons and Earth. The Confederation itself—the government—really doesn't care. Why should it? But the people do—or would."

"Oh," Norma said, "oh…of course."

"That's right," Dr. Haenlingen said. "They hear about freedom, and all the rest, as soon as they're old enough to hear about anything. It's part of every subject they study in school, it's part of the world they live in, it's like the air they breathe. They can't question it. They can't even think about it."

"And, of course, if they hear about Fruyling's World—"

"There won't be any way to disguise the fact," Dr. Haenlingen said. "In the long run, there never is. And the fact will shock them into action. As long as they continue to live in that air of freedom and justice and equality under the law, they'll want to stop what we're doing here. They'll have to."

"I see," Norma said. "Of course."

Dr. Haenlingen, still looking out at the world below, smiled faintly. "Slavery," she said, "is such an ugly word."

CHAPTER TWO

THE COMMONS ROOM of the Third Building of City One was a large affair, whose three bare metal walls enclosed more space than any other single living-quarters room in the Building; but the presence of the fourth wall made it seem tiny. That wall was nearly all window, a non-shatterable clear plastic immensely superior to that laboratory material, glass. It displayed a single unbroken sweep of forty feet, and it looked down on the forests of Fruyling's World from a height of sixteen stories. Men new to the Third Building usually sat with their backs to that enormous window, and even the eldest inhabitants usually placed their chairs somehow out of line with it, and looked instead at the walls, at their companions, or at their own hands.

Fruyling's World was disturbing, and not only because of the choking profusion of forest that always seemed to threaten the isolated clusters of human residence. A man could get used to forests. But at any moment, looking down or out across the gray-green vegetation, that man might catch sight of a native—an Elder, perhaps heading slowly out toward the Birth huts hidden in the lashing trees, or a group of Small Ones being herded into the Third Building itself for their training. It was hard, perhaps impossible, to get used to that. When you had to see the natives you steeled yourself for the job. When you didn't have to see them you counted yourself lucky and called yourself relaxed.

It wasn't that the natives were hideous, either. Their very name had been given to them by men in a kind of affectionate mockery, since they weren't advanced enough even to have such a group-name of their own as "the people." They were called Alberts, after a half-forgotten character in a mistily remembered comic strip dating back before space travel, before the true beginnings of Confederation history. If you ignored the single, Cyclopean eye, the rather musty smell and a few other even more minor details, they looked rather like two-legged alligators four feet tall, green as jewels, with hopeful grins on their faces and an awkward, waddling walk like a penguin's. Seen without preconceptions they might have been called cute.

But no man on Fruyling's World could see the Alberts without preconceptions. They were not Alberts. They were slaves, as the men were masters. And slavery, named and accepted, has traditionally been harder on the master than the slave.

John Dodd, twenty-seven years old, master, part of the third generation, arranged his chair carefully so that it faced the door of the Commons Room, letting the light from the great window illumine the back of his head. He clasped his hands in his lap in a single, nervous gesture, never noticing that the light gave him a faint saint-like halo about his feathery hair. His companion took another chair, set it at right angles to Dodd's and gave it long and thoughtful consideration, as if the act of sitting down were something new and untried.

"It's good to be off-duty," Dodd said violently. "Good. Not to have to see them—not to have to think about them until tomorrow."

The standing man, shorter than Dodd and built heavily, actually turned and looked out at the window. "And then tomorrow what do you do?" he asked. "Give up your job? You're just letting the thing get you, Johnny."

"I'd give up my job in twenty seconds if I thought it would do any good," Dodd said. He shook his head. "I give up a job here in the Buildings, and then what do I do? Go out and starve in the jungle? Nobody's done it, nobody's ever done it."

"Well?" the squat man said. "Is that an excuse?"

Dodd sighed. "Those who work get fed," he said. "And housed. And clothed. And—heaven help us—entertained, by 3D tapes older than our fathers are. If a man didn't work he'd get—cast out. Cut off."

"There's more than 3D tapes," the squat man said, and grinned.

"Sure." Dodd's voice was tired. "But think about it for a minute, Albin. Do you know what we've got here?"

"We've got a nice, smooth setup," Albin said. "No worries, no fights, a job to do and a place to do it in, time to relax, time to have fun. It's okay."

There was a little silence. Dodd's voice seemed more distant. "Marxian economics," he said. "Perfect Marxian economics, on a world that would make old Karl spin in his grave like an electron."

"I guess so," Albin said. "History's not my field. But—given the setup, what else could there be? What other choice have you got?"

"I don't know." Again a silence. Dodd's hands unclasped. He made a gesture as if he were sweeping something away from his face. "There ought to be something else. Even on Earth, even before the Confederation, there were conscientious objectors."

"History again," Albin said. He walked a few steps toward the window. "Anyhow, that was for war."

"I don't know," Dodd said. His hands went back into his lap, and his eyes closed. He spoke, now, like a man in a dream. "There used to be all kinds of jobs. I guess there still are, in the Confederation. On Earth. Back home where none of us have ever been." He repeated the words like an echo: "Back home." In the silence nothing interrupted him. Behind his head light poured in from the giant window. "A man could choose his own job," he went on, in the same tone. "He could be a factory worker or a professor or a truck-driver or a musician or—a lot of jobs. A man didn't have to work at one, whether he wanted to or not."

"All right," Albin said. "Okay. So suppose you had your choice. Suppose every job in every damn history you've ever heard of was open to you. Just what would you pick? Make a choice. Go ahead, make—"

"It isn't funny, Albin," Dodd said woodenly. "It isn't a game."

"Okay, it isn't," Albin said. "So make it a game. Just for a minute. Think over all the jobs you can and make a choice. You don't like being here, do you? You don't like working with the Alberts. So where would you like to be? What would you like to do?" He came back to the chair, his eyes on Dodd, and sat suddenly down, his elbows on his knees and his chin cupped in his hands, facing Dodd like a gnome out of prehistory. "Go on," he said. "Make a choice."

"Okay," Dodd said without opening his eyes. His voice became more distant, dreamlike. "Okay," he said again. "I—there isn't one job, but maybe a kind of job. Something to do with growing things." There was a pause. "I'd like to work somewhere growing things. I'd like to work with plants. They're all right, plants. They don't make you feel anything." The voice stopped.

"Plants?" Albin hooted gigantically. "Good God, think about it! You're stuck on a planet that's over seventy percent plant life—trees and weeds and jungles all over the land and even mats of green stuff covering the oceans and riding on the rivers—a planet that's just about nothing but plants, a king-sized hothouse for every kind of leaf and blade and flower and fruit you could ever dream up—"

"It's not the same," Dodd said.

"You," Albin said, "are out of your head. So if you're crazy for plants, go grow them in your spare time. If you've got a window in your room you can put up a window box. If not, something else. Me, I think it's damn silly. With the plants all around here, what's the sense of growing more? But if you like it, it's clear that Fruyling's World is ready to provide it for you."

"As a hobby," Dodd said flatly.

"Well, then, a hobby," Albin said. "If you're interested in it."

"Interested." The word was like an echo. A silence fell. Albin's eyes studied Dodd, the thin face and the play of light on the hair. After a while he shrugged.

"So it isn't plants," he said. "It isn't any more than the Alberts and working with them. You want to do anything to get away from them—anything that won't remind you that you have to go back."

"Sure," Dodd said. "Sure I do. So do all of us."

"Not me," Albin said instantly. "Not me, brother. I get my food and my clothing and my shelter, just like good old Marx, I guess, says I should. I'm a trainer for the Alberts, supportive work in the refining process, and some day I'll be a master trainer and get a little more pay, a little more status, you know?" He grinned and sat straight. "What the hell," he said, "It's a job. It pays my way. And there's enough leisure time for fun—and when I say fun I don't mean 3D tapes, Dodd. I really don't."

"But you—"

"Look," Albin said. "That's what's wrong with you, kid. You talk as if we all had nothing to do but work and watch tapes. What you need is a little education—a little real education—and I'm the one to give it to you."

Dodd opened his eyes. They looked very large and flat,

like the eyes of a jungle animal. "I don't need education," he said. "And I don't need hobbies. I need to get off this planet, that's all. I need to stop working with the Alberts. I need to stop being a master and start being a man again."

Albin sighed. "Slavery," he said. "You think of slavery and it all rises up in front of you—Greece, India, China, Rome, England, the United States—all the past before the Confederation, all the different slaves." He grinned again. "You think it's terrible, don't you?"

"It is terrible," Dodd said. "It's—they're people, just like us. They have a right to their own lives."

"Sure they do," Albin said. "They have the right to—oh, to starve and die in that forest out there, for instance. And work out a lot of primitive rituals, and go through all the Stone Age motions for thousands of years until they develop civilization like you and me. Instead of being kept nice and warm and comfortable and taken care of, and taught things, by the evil old bastards like—well, like you and me again. Right?"

"They have rights," Dodd said stubbornly. "They have rights of their own."

"Sure they do," Albin agreed with great cheerfulness. "How'd you like it if they got some of them? Dodd, maybe you'd like to see them starve? Because it's going to be a long, long time before they develop anything like a solid civilization, kiddo. And in the meantime a lot of them are going to die of things we can prevent. Right? And how'd you like that, Dodd? How would you like that?"

Dodd hesitated. "We ought to help them," he muttered.

"Well," Albin said cheerfully, "that's what we are doing. Keeping them alive, for instance. And teaching them."

"Teaching," Dodd said. Again his voice had the faintly mocking sound of an echo. "And what are we teaching them? Push this button for us. Watch this process for us. If anything changes push this button. Dig here. Carry there." He paused. "Wonderful—for us. But what good does it do them?"

"We've got to live, too," Albin said.

Dodd stared. "At their expense?"

"It's a living," Albin said casually, shrugging. "But I'm serious. One good dose of real enjoyment will cure you, friend. One good dose of fun—by which, kiddo, I mean plain ordinary old sex, such as can be had any free evening around here—and you'll stop being depressed and worried. Uncle Albin Cendar's Priceless Old Recipe, kiddo, and don't argue with me…it works."

Dodd said nothing at all. After a few seconds his eyes slowly closed and he sat like a statue in the room.

Albin, watching him, whistled inaudibly under his breath. A minute went by silently. The light in the room began to diminish.

"Sun's going down," Albin offered.

There was no response. Albin got up again and went to the window.

"Maybe you're right," he said with his back to Dodd's still figure. "There ought to be some way of getting people off-planet, people who just don't want to stay here."

"Do you know why there isn't?" Dodd's voice was a shock stronger than before.

"Sure I know," Albin said. "There's—"

"Slavery," Dodd said. "Oh, sure, maybe somebody knows about it, but it's got to be kept quiet. And if anybody got back—well, look."

"Don't bother me with it." Albin's voice was suddenly less sure.

"Look," Dodd said. "The Confederation needs the metal. It exists pure here, and in quantity. But if they knew, really knew, how we mined and smelted and purified it and got it ready for shipment…"

"So suppose somebody goes back," Albin said. "Suppose somebody talks. What difference does it make? It's just rumor, nothing official. No, the reason nobody goes back is cargo space, pure and simple. We need every inch of cargo space for the shipments."

"If somebody goes back," Dodd said, "the people will know. Not the government, not the businesses, the people. And the people don't like slavery, Albin. No matter how necessary a government finds it. No matter what kind of a jerry-built defense you can put up for it."

"Don't be silly," Albin said. There was less conviction in his voice; he looked out at the sunset as if he were trying to reassure himself.

"Nobody's allowed to leave," Dodd said, more quietly. "We're—they're taking every precaution they can. But some day—maybe some day, Albin—the people are going to find out in spite of every precaution." He sat straighter. "And then it'll all be over. Then they'll be wiped out, Albin. Wiped out."

"They need us," Albin said uncertainly. "They can't do without us."

Dodd swung round to face him. The sunset was a deepening blaze in the Commons Room. "Wait and find out," he said in a voice that suddenly rang off the metal walls. "Wait and find out."

After a long time Albin said. "Damn it, what you need is education. A cure. Fun. What I've been saying." He paused and took a breath. "How about it, Dodd?"

Dodd didn't move. Another second passed. "All right, Albin," he said slowly, at last. "I'll think about it. I'll think about it."

CHAPTER THREE

THE SLEEPING ROOM for the Small Ones was, by comparison with the great Commons Room only the masters inhabited, a tiny place. It had only the smallest of windows, so placed as to allow daylight without any sight of the outside; the windows were plastic-sheeted slits high up on the metal walls, no more. The room was, at best, dim, during the day, but that hardly mattered. During the day the room was empty. Only at night, when the soft artificial lights went on, shedding the glow from their wall-shielded tubes, was the room fit for normal vision. There were no decorations, of course, and no chairs. The Alberts had no use for chairs, and decorations were a refinement no master had yet bothered to think of. The Alberts were hardly taught to appreciate such things in any case—that was not what they had come to learn. It was not useful.

The floor of the room was covered with soft leaves striped a glossy brown over the pervasive gray-green of the planet's foliage. These served as a soft mat for sleeping, and were also the staple food of the Alberts. These were not disturbed to find their food strewn in such irregular heaps and drifts across the metal floor. In their birth sacs, they had lived by ingestion from the floor of the forest, and, later, they had been so fed in the Birth Huts to which the Elders had taken them, and where they had been cleaned and served and taught, among other matters, English.

What they had been taught was, at any rate, English of a sort, bearing within it the seeds of a more complex tongue, and having its roots far back in the pre-space centuries, when missionaries had first begun to visit strange lands. Men had called it pidgin and Beche-le-mer and a hundred different names in a hundred different variations. Here, the masters called it English. The Alberts called it words, and nothing more.

Now, after sunset, they filed in, thirty or so jewel-green cyclopean alligators at the end of their first day of training, waddling clumsily past the doorway and settled with a grateful, crouching squat on the leaves that served as bed and food. None were bothered by the act of sitting on the leaves. For one thing, they had no concept of dirt. In the second place, they were rather remarkably clean. They had neither sex organs, in any human sense of the word, or specific organs of evacuation. Their entire elimination was gaseous. Air ducts in the room would draw off the waste products, and the Alberts never noticed them. They had, in fact, no conception of evacuation as a process, since to them the entire procedure was invisible and impalpable.

The last of them filed in, and the masters—two of them, carrying long metal tubes—shut the door. The Alberts were alone. The door's clang was followed by other sounds as the lock was thrown. The new noises, and the strangeness of bare metal walls and artificial light, still novel after only a single day's training, gave rise to something very like a panic, and a confused babble of voices arose from the crowd.

"What is this?"

"What place is this?"

"It is a training place."

"My name Hortat. My name Hortat."

"What is training?"

"There is food here."

"What place is this?"

"Where are elders?"

"Are masters here?"

"My food."

"Is this a place for sleeping?"

"Training is to do what a master says. Training—"

"There are no elders. My name Hortat."

"My place."

"My food."

"Where is this?"

"Where is this place?"

Like the stirring of a child in sleep, the panic lasted only a little while, and gave way to an apathetic peace. Here and there an Albert munched on a leaf, holding it up before his wide mouth in the pose of a giant squirrel. Others sat quietly looking at the walls or the door or the window, or at nothing. One, whose name was Cadnan, stirred briefly and dropped the leaf he was eating and turned to the Albert next to him.

"Marvor," he said. "Are you troubled?"

Marvor seemed slighter than Cadnan, and his single eye larger, but both looked very much alike to humans, as members of other races, and particularly such races as the human in question judges inferior, are prone to do. "I do not know what happens," he said in a flat tone. "I do not know what is this place, or what we do."

"This is the place of masters," Cadnan said. "We train here, and we work here, and live here. It is the rule of the masters."

"Yet I do not know," Marvor said. "This training is a hard thing, and the work is also hard when it comes."

Cadnan closed his eye for a second, to relax, but he found he wanted to talk. His first day in the world of the masters had been too confusing for him to order it into any sensible structure. Conversation, of whatever kind, was a release, and might provide more facts. Cadnan was hungry for facts.

He opened his eye again.

"It is what the masters say," he told Marvor. "The

masters say we do a thing, and we do it. This is right."

Marvor bent toward him. "Why is it right?" he asked.

"Because the masters say it is right," Cadnan told him, with the surprised air of a person explaining the obvious. "The elders, too, say it before we come to this place." He added the final sentence like a totally unnecessary clincher— unimportant by comparison with the first reason, but adding a little weight of its own, and making the whole story even more satisfying.

Marvor, however, didn't seem satisfied. "The masters always speak truth," he said. "Is this what you tell me?"

"It is true," Cadnan said flatly.

Marvor reflected for a second. "It may be," he said at last. He turned away, found a leaf and began to munch on it slowly. Cadnan picked up his own leaf quite automatically, and it was several seconds before he realized that Marvor had ended the conversation. He didn't want it to end. Talk, he told himself dimly, was a good thing.

"Marvor," he said, "do you question the masters?" It was a difficult sentence to frame. The idea itself would never have occurred to him without Marvor's prodding, and it seemed now no more than the wildest possible flight of fancy. But Marvor, turning, did not treat it fancifully at all.

"I question all," he said soberly. "It is good to question all."

"But the masters—" Cadnan said.

Marvor turned away again without answering.

Cadnan stared at his leaf for a time. His mind was troubled, and there were no ready solutions in it. He was not of the temperament to fasten himself to easy solutions. He had instead to hammer out his ideas slowly and carefully. Then when he had reached a conclusion of some kind, he had confidence in it and knew it would last.

Marvor was just the same—but perhaps there had been

something wrong with him from the beginning. Otherwise, Cadnan realized, he would never have questioned the masters. None of the Alberts questioned the masters, any more than they questioned their food or the air they breathed.

After a time Marvor spoke again. "I am different," he said. "I am not like others."

Cadnan thought this too obvious to be worth reply, and waited.

"The elders tell me in the hut I am different," Marvor went on. "When they come to bring food they tell me this."

Cadnan took a deep breath of the air. It was, of course, scented with the musk of the Alberts, but Cadnan could not recognize it. Like his fellows, he had no sense of smell. "Different is not good," he said, perceiving a lesson.

"You find out how different I am." Marvor sat very still. His voice was still flat but the tone carried something very like a threat. Cadnan, involved in his own thinking, ignored it.

"The masters are big and we are small," he said slowly. "The masters know better than we know."

"That is silliness," Marvor said instantly. "I want things. They make me do training. Why can I not do what I want to do?"

"Maybe," Cadnan said with care, "it is bad."

Marvor made a hissing sound. "Maybe they are bad," he said. "Maybe the masters and the elders are bad."

Matters had gone so far that even this thought found a tentative lodgment in Cadnan's mind. But, almost at once, it was rejected as a serious concept. "They give us leaves to eat," he said. "They keep us here, warm and dry in this place. How is this bad?"

Marvor closed his eye and made the hissing sound again; it was equivalent to a laugh of rejection. He turned among the leaves and found enough room to lie down. In a few seconds he was either asleep or imitating sleep very well. Cadnan looked at him hopefully, and then turned away. A female was watching him from the other side, her eyes wide and unblinking.

"You ask many questions," the female said. "You speak much."

Cadnan blinked his eye at her. "I want to learn," he said.

"Is it good to learn?" the female asked. The question made Cadnan uncomfortable. Who knew, for certain, what was good? He knew he would have to think it out for a long time. But the female wanted an answer.

"It is good," he said casually.

The female accepted that with quiet passivity. "My name is Dara," she said. "It is what I am called."

Cadnan said, "I am Cadnan." He found himself tired, and Dara apparently saw this and withdrew, leaving him to sleep.

But his sleep was troubled, and it seemed a long time before day came and the door opened again to show the masters with their strange metal tubes standing outside in the corridor.

CHAPTER FOUR

'I'M NOT going to take no for an answer."

Albin stood in the doorway of his room, slouching against the metal lintel and looking even more like a gnome. Dodd sighed softly and got up from the single chair. "I'm not anxious for a party," he said. "All I want to do is go to sleep."

"At nine o'clock?" Albin shook his head.

"Maybe I'm tired."

"You're not tired," Albin said. "You're scared. You're scared of what you might find out there in the cold, cruel world, friend. You're scared of parties and strange people and noise. You want to be left alone to brood, right?"

"No, I—"

"But I'm not going to leave you alone to brood," Albin said. "Because I'm your friend. And brooding isn't good for you. It's brooding that's got you into such a state—where you worry about growing things, for heaven's sake, and about freedom and silly things like that." Albin grinned. "What you've got to do is stop worrying, and I know how to get you to do that, kiddo. I really do."

"Sure you do," Dodd said, and his voice began to rise. He went to the bed, walked along its length to the window, as he talked, never facing Albin. "You know how to make me feel just fine, no worries at all, no complications, just a nice, simple life. With nothing at all in it, Albin. Nothing at all."

"Now, come on—" Albin began.

"Nothing," Dodd said. "Go to parties, drink, meet a girl, forget, go right on forgetting, and then one day you wake up and it's over and what have you got?"

"Parties," Albin said. "Girls. Drinks. What else is there?"

"A lot," Dodd said. "I want— Hell...I don't know what I want. Too much. Too many ideas...trapped here being a master, and that's no good."

"Dodd," Albin said, in what was almost a worried tone, "what the hell are you talking about?"

"Being a master," Dodd said. "There shouldn't be masters. Or slaves. Just—beings, able to do what they want to do...what makes me any better than the Alberts, anyhow?"

"The Belbis beam, for one thing," Albin said. "Position, power, protection, punishment. What makes anybody better than anybody else?"

"But that's the point—don't you see?'

Albin stood upright, massaging his arm. "What I see is a case of worry," he said, "and as a doctor I have certain responsibilities. I've got to take care of that case of worries, and I'm not going to take no for an answer."

"Leave me alone," Dodd said. "Just do me a favor. Leave me alone."

"Come with me," Albin said. "This once. Look—what can you lose? Just once can't hurt you—you can do all the brooding you want to do some other time. Give me a present. Come to the party with me."

"I don't like parties."

"And I don't like going alone," Albin said. "So do me a favor."

"Where is it?" Dodd asked after a second.

Albin beamed. "Psych division," he said. "Come on."

The metal door was festooned with paper drapery in red and blue. Dodd turned before they got to it, standing about five feet down the corridor. "How did you find out about a party in Psych division?" he asked.

Albin shrugged. "I'm an active type," he said. "I've got friends all over. You'd be surprised how many friends a man can have, Dodd, if he goes to parties. If he meets people instead of brooding."

"All right," Dodd said. "I'm here, aren't I? You've convinced me—stop the propaganda."

"Sure." Albin went up to the door and knocked. From inside they could hear a dim babble of voices. After a second he knocked again, more loudly.

A voice rose above the hum. "Who's there?"

"A friend," Albin said. "The password is Haenlingen-on-fire.

The voice broke into laughter. "Oh," it said. It was now distinguishingly a female voice. "It's you, Cendar. But hold it down on the Haenlingen stuff. She's supposed to be arriving."

"At a party?" Albin said. "She's a hundred and twelve—older than that. What does she want with parties? Don't be silly."

The door opened. A slim, blonde girl stood by it, her mouth still grinning. "Cendar, I mean it," she said. "You watch out. One of these days you're going to get into trouble."

Behind her the hum had risen to a chorus of mad clatter, conversation, laughter, song—the girl dragged Albin and Dodd inside and shut the door. "I'm always in trouble," Albin was saying. "It keeps life interesting." But it was hard to hear him, hard to hear any single voice in the swell of noise.

"Thank God for soundproofing," the girl said. "We can do whatever we like and there's no noise out there."

"The drapes give you away," Albin said.

"Let the drapes give us away," the girl said. "We're entitled to have quiet little gatherings, right? And who knows what goes on behind the drapes?"

"Right," Albin said. "You are right. You are absolutely, incredibly, stunningly right. And to prove how right you are I'm going to do you a favor."

"What kind of favor?" the girl said with mock suspicion.

"Greta," Albin said, "I'm going to introduce you to a nice young man."

"You don't know any nice young men."

"I know this one," Albin said. "Greta Forzane...Johnny Dodd. Take good care of him, kiddo—he needs it."

"What do you mean, good care of him?" she said. But Albin was gone, into the main body of the party, a melee confused enough so that he was lost in twenty steps. Greta turned back almost hopeless eyes.

A second passed.

"You a friend of Cendar's?" Greta asked.

Dodd blinked and came back to her, "Oh, Albin," he said. "We're—acquaintances."

"Friends," Greta said firmly. "That's nice. He's such a nice guy—I bet you are, too." She smiled and took his arm. Her hand was slightly warm and very dry. Dodd took his first real look at her. She seemed shining, somehow, as if the hair had been lacquered, the face sprayed with a clear polish. The picture she made was vaguely unpleasant, and a little threatening.

"A nice guy?" he said. "I wouldn't know, Miss Forzane."

"Oh, come on, now," she said. "The name is Greta. And you're Johnny—right?"

"...Right," Dodd answered.

"You know," Greta said, "you're cute."

Behind her the party was still going on, but its volume seemed to have diminished a little. Or maybe, Dodd thought, he was getting used to it. "You're cute too," he said awkwardly, not knowing any more what he did want to do, or where he wanted to be. Her grasp on his arm was the main fact in the world.

"Thanks," she said. "Here."

And as suddenly as that she was in his arms, plastered up against him, pressed to him as tightly as he could imagine, her mouth on his, her hands locked behind his neck. He was choking, he couldn't breathe, he couldn't move...

The door behind him opened and shoved him gently across his back.

He fell, and he fell on top of her.

It seemed as if the entire party had stopped to watch him. There was no noise. There was no sound at all. He climbed to his feet to face the eyes and found they were not on him, but behind him.

A tiny white-haired woman stood there, her mouth one thin line of disapproval. "Well," she said. "Having a good time?"

In Dodd's mind, then and later, the sign began.

That was, as far as he could ever remember, the first second he had even seen it. It was there, behind his eyes, blinking on and off, like a neon sign. Sometimes he paid no attention to it, but it was always there, always telling him the same thing.

This is the end.
This is the end.
This is the end.

He looked into that ancient grim face and the sign began. And from then on it never stopped, never stopped at all—

Until, of course, the end.

PUBLIC OPINION ONE

Being an excerpt from a speech delivered by Grigor Pellasin (Citizen, white male, age forty-seven, two arrests for

Disorderly Conduct, occupation variable, residence variable)
in the district of Hyde Park, city of London, country of
England, planet Earth of the Confederation, in the year of the
Confederation two hundred and ten, on May fourteenth,
from two-thirty-seven P. M. (Greenwich) until three-forty-six
P. M. (Greenwich), no serious incidents reported.

They all talk about equality, friends, and you know what equality is? Equality is a license to rob you blind and steal you blind, to cut you up and leave the pieces for the garbage collector, to stuff what's left of you down an oubliette, friend, and forget about you. That's what equality is, friends, and don't you let them tell you any different.

Why, years ago there used to be servants, people who did what you told them. And the servants got liberated, friends, they all got freedom and equality so they were just like us. Maybe you can remember about those servants, because they're all in the history books, and the historical novels, and maybe you do a little light reading now and then, am I right about that?

Well, sir, those servants got themselves liberated, and do you think they liked it? Do you think they liked being free and equal?

Oh, don't ask the government, friends, because the government is going to tell you they liked it just fine, going to tell you they loved it being just like everybody else, free and equal and liberated at last.

The government's going to tell you a lot of things, and my advice is, friends, my advice is do some looking and listening for yourself and think it all out to the right conclusions. Otherwise you're just letting the government do all your thinking for you and that's something you don't want.

No, friends, you do your own thinking and you figure out whether they liked being free, these servants.

You know what being free meant for them?

It meant being out of work.

And how do you think they liked that?

Now, maybe here among us today, among you kind people listening to what I've got to say to you, maybe there are one or two who've been out of work during their lifetimes. Am I right? Well, friends, you tell the others here what it felt like.

It felt hopeless and dragged-out and like something you'd never want to go through again, am I right?

Of course I'm right, friends. But there was nothing you could do about being out of work. If you were out of work that was that, and you were through, no chance, no place to move.

These servants, friends, they liked being servants. I know that's hard to believe because everybody's been telling you different all your lives, but you just do a little independent thinking, the way I have, and you'll see. It was a good job, being a servant. It was steady and dependable and you knew where you stood.

Better than being out of work? You bet your last credit, you bet your very last ounce of bounce on that, friends.

And better than a lot of other things, too. They were safe and warm and happy, and they felt fine.

And then a lot of busybodies came along and liberated them.

Well, friends, some of them went right back and asked to be servants again—they did so. It's a historical fact. But that was no good. The machines had taken over and there was no room for them.

They were liberated for good.

And the lesson you learn from that, friends, is just this: don't go around liberating people until you know what they want. Maybe they're happier the way they are.

Now, out on a far planet there's a strange race. Maybe you've heard about them, because they work for us, they help get us the metals we need to keep going. They're part of the big line of supply that keeps us all alive, you and me both.

And there are some people talking about liberating those creatures, too, which aren't even human beings. They're green and they got one eye apiece, and they don't talk English except a little, or any Confederation tongue.

Yet even so there are people who want to liberate those creatures.

Now, you sit back and think a minute. Do those creatures want to be liberated? Is it like liberating you and me, who know what's what and can think and make decisions? Because being free and equal means voting and everything else. Do you want these green creatures voting in the same assemblies as yours?

If it were cruel to keep them the way they are, working on their own world and being fed and kept warm and safe, why, I'd say go ahead and liberate them. But what's cruel about it, friends?

They're safe—safer than they would be on their own.

They're fed well and kept warm.

And remember those servants, friends. Maybe the greenies like their life, too. It's their world and their metal— they have a right to help send it along.

You don't want to act hastily, friends, now do you?

My advice to you is this: just let the greenies alone. Just let them be, the way they want to be, and don't go messing around where there's no need to mess around. Because if anybody starts to do that, why, it can lead to trouble, friends, to a whole lot of unnecessary bother and trouble.

Am I right?

CHAPTER FIVE

"I DON'T MIND parties, Norma, not ordinary parties. But that one didn't look like an ordinary party."

Norma stood her ground in front of the desk. This, after all, was important. "But, Dr. Haenlingen, we—"

"Don't try to persuade me," the little old woman said sharply. "Don't try to cozen me into something. I know all the tricks, Norma. I invented a good third of them, and it's been a long time since I had to use a textbook to remember the rest."

"I'm not trying to persuade you of anything." The woman wouldn't listen, that was the whole trouble. In the harsh bright light of morning she sat like a stone statue, casting a shadow of black on the polished desk. This was Dr. Haenlingen—and how did you talk to Dr. Haenlingen? But it was important, Norma reminded herself again. It was perfectly possible that the entire group of people at the party would be downgraded, or at the least get marked down on their records. "But we weren't doing anything harmful. If you have a party you've got to expect people to—oh, to get over-enthusiastic, maybe. But certainly there was nothing worth getting angry about. There was—"

"I'm sure you've thought all this out," Dr. Haenlingen said tightly. "You seem to have your case well prepared, and it would be a pleasure to listen to you."

"But—"

"Unfortunately," the woman continued in a voice like steel. "I have a great deal of work to do this morning."

"Dr. Haenlingen—"

"I'm sorry," she said, but she didn't sound sorry in the

least. Her eyes went down to a pile of papers on the desk. A second passed.

"You've got to listen to me," Norma said. "What you're doing is unfair."

Dr. Haenlingen didn't look up. "Oh?"

"They were just—having fun," Norma said. "There was nothing wrong, nothing at all. You happened to come in at a bad moment, but it didn't mean anything, there wasn't anything going on that should have bothered you..."

"Perhaps not," Dr. Haenlingen said. "Unfortunately, what bothers me is not reducible to rule."

"But you're going to act on it," Norma said. "You're going to—"

"Yes?" Dr. Haenlingen said. "What am I going to do?"

"Well, you—"

"Downgrade the persons who were there?" Dr. Haenlingen asked. "Enter remarks in the permanent records? Prevent promotion? Just what am I supposed to have in mind?"

"Well, I thought—I—"

"I plan," Dr. Haenlingen said, "nothing whatever. Not just at present. I want to think about what I saw, about the people I saw. At present, nothing more."

There was a little silence, Norma felt herself relax. Then she asked: "At present?"

Dr. Haenlingen looked up at her, the eyes ice-cold and direct. "What action I determine to take," she said, "will be my responsibility. Mine alone. I do not intend to discuss it or to attempt to justify it, to you or to anyone."

"Yes, Dr. Haenlingen." Norma stood awkwardly. "Thank you—"

"Don't thank me—yet," Dr. Haenlingen said. "Go and do your own work. I've got quite a lot to oversee here." She went back to her papers. Norma turned, stopped and then walked to the door. At the door she turned again but Dr. Haenlingen was paying no visible attention to her. She opened the door, went out and closed it behind her.

In the corridor she took one deep breath and then another.

The trouble was, you couldn't depend on the woman to do anything. She meant exactly what she had said: "For the present." And who could tell what might happen later?

Norma headed for her own cubicle, where she ignored the papers and the telephone messages waiting for her and reached for the intercom button instead. She pushed it twice and a voice said:

"What happened?"

"It's not good, Greta," Norma said. "It's—well, undecided, anyhow. We've got that much going for us."

"Undecided?" the voice asked.

"She said she wouldn't do anything—yet, but she left it open."

"Oh. Lord. Oh, my."

Norma nodded at the intercom speaker. "That's right. Anything's possible—you know what she's like."

"Oh, Lord. Do I."

"And—Greta, why did you have to be there, right by the door, with that strange type—as if it had been set up for her? Right in front of her eyes…"

"An accident," Greta said. "A pure accident. When she walked in, when I saw her, believe me, Norma, my blood ran absolutely cold. Temperature of ice, or something colder than ice."

"Just that one look, just that one long look around." Norma said, "and she was gone. As if she'd memorized us, every one of us, filed the whole thing away and didn't need to see any more."

"I would have explained. But there wasn't any time."

"I know," Norma said. "Greta, who was he, anyhow?"

"Him?" Greta said. "Who knows? A friend of Cendar's—you know Cendar, don't you?"

"Albin Cendar?"

"That's the one. He—"

"But he's not from Psych." Norma said.

"Neither is his friend, I guess," Greta said. "But they come over, you know that—Cendar's always around."

"And you had to invite them..."

"Invite?" Greta said. "I didn't invite anybody. They were there, that's all. Cendar always shows up. You know that."

"Great," Norma said. "So last night he had to bring a friend and the friend got grabby—"

"No," Greta said. "He was—well, confused maybe. Never been to a party of ours before, or anyhow not that I remember. I was trying to—loosen him up."

"You loosened everybody up," Norma said.

There was a silence.

"I'm sorry," Norma said. "All right. You couldn't have known—"

"I didn't know anything," Greta's voice said. "She was there, that's all."

"I wonder whether Dr. Haenlingen knew him," Norma said. "The new one, I mean."

"His name was Johnny something," Greta said.

"We'll just have to wait and find out," Norma said. "Whatever she's going to do, there isn't any way to stop it. I did the best I could—"

"Sure you did," Greta said. "We know that. Sure."

"Cendar and his friends—" Norma began.

"Oh, forget about that," Greta said. "Who cares about, them?"

CHAPTER SIX

THE PARTY had meant nothing, nothing at all, and Albin told himself he could forget all about it.

If Haenlingen wanted to take any action, he insisted, she'd take it against her own division. The Psych people would get most of it. Why, she probably didn't even know who Albin Cendar was...

But the Psych division knew a lot they weren't supposed to know. Maybe she would even...

Forget about it, Albin told himself. He closed his eyes for a second and concentrated on his work. That, at least, was something to keep him from worrying. The whole process of training was something he could use in forgetting all about the party, and Haenlingen, and possible consequences... He took a few breaths and forced his mind away from all of that, back to the training.

Training was a dreary waste of time, as a matter of fact— except that it happened to be necessary. There was no doubt of that. Without sufficient manual labor, the metal would not be dug, the smelters would not run, and the purifying stages and the cooling stages and even the shipping itself would simply stop. Automation would have solved everything, but automation was expensive. The Alberts were cheap—so Fruyling's World used Alberts instead of transistors and cryogenic relays.

And if you were going to use Alberts at all, Albin thought, you sure as hell had to train them. God alone knew what harm they could do, left alone in a wilderness of delicate machinery without any instructions.

All the same, "dreary" was the word for it. (An image of

Dr. Haenlingen's frozen face floated into his mind. He pushed it away. It was morning. It was time for work.)

He met Derban at the turn in the corridor, perhaps fifty feet before the Alberts' door. That wasn't strictly according to the rules, and Albin knew it. He had learned the code as early as anyone else. But the rules were for emergencies—and emergencies didn't happen any more. The Alberts weren't about to revolt.

He was carrying his Belbis beam, of course. The little metal tube didn't look like much, but it was guaranteed to stop anything short of a spaceship in its tracks, and by the very simple method of making holes. The Belbis beam would make holes in nearly anything: Alberts, people or most materials. It projected a quarter-inch beam of force in as near a straight line as Einsteinian physics would allow, and it was extremely efficient. Albin had been practicing with it for three years, twice a week.

Everybody did. Not that there's ever been a chance to use it.

And there wasn't going to be a chance, Albin decided. He exchanged a word or two absently with Derban and they went to the door together. Albin reached for the door but Derban's big brown hand was already on it. He grinned and swung the door open.

Air conditioning had done something to minimize the reek inside, but not much. Albin devoted most of his attention to keeping his face a complete mask. The last thing he wanted was to retch—not in front of the Alberts, who didn't really exist for him, but in front of Derban. And the party (which he wasn't going to think about) hadn't left his stomach in perfect shape.

The Alberts, seeing these masters enter, stirred and rose. Albin barked at them in a voice that was only very slightly choked: "Form a line. Form a line."

The Alberts milled around, quite obviously uncertain what a line was. Albin gripped his beam tighter, not because it was a weapon but just because he needed something handy to take out his anger on.

"Damn it," he said tightly, "a line. Form a straight line."

"It's only their second day," Derban said in a low voice. "Give them time." Albin could barely hear him over the confused babble of the Alberts. He shook his head and felt a new stab of anger.

"One behind the other," he told the milling crowd. "A line, a straight line."

After a little more confusion, Albin was satisfied. He sighed heavily and beckoned with his beam. The Alberts started forward, through the door and out into the corridor.

Albin went before, Derban behind, falling naturally into step. They came to the great elevator and Albin pushed a stud. The door slid open.

The Alberts, though, didn't want to go in. They huddled, looking at the elevator with big round eyes, muttering to themselves and to each other. Derban spoke up calmly: "This is the same room you were in yesterday. It won't hurt you. Just go through the door. It's all right." But the words had very little effect. A few of the Alberts moved closer and then, discovering that they were alone, hurriedly moved back again. The elevator door remained open, waiting.

Albin, ready to shriek with rage by now, felt a touch at his arm. One of the Alberts was standing near him, looking up. Its eye blinked, then it spoke.

"Why does the room move?"

The voice was not actually unpleasant, but its single eye stared at Albin, making him uncomfortable. He told himself not to blow up. Calm. Calm.

"The room moves because it moves," he said, a little too quickly. "Because the masters tell it to move. What do you want to know for?"

"I want to learn," the Albert said calmly.

"Well, don't ask questions," Albin said. He kept one eye on the shifting mob. "If there's anything good for you to know, you'll be told. Meanwhile, just don't ask any questions."

The Albert looked downcast. "Can I learn without questions?"

Albin's control snapped. "Damn it, you'll learn what you have to!" he yelled. "You don't have to ask questions—you're a slave. A slave! Get that through your green head and shut up!"

The tone had two effects. First, it made the Albert near him move back, staring at him still with that single bright eye. Second, the others started for the elevator, apparently pushed more by the tone than the words. A master was angry. That, they judged, meant trouble. Acceding to his wishes was the safest thing to do.

And so, in little, frightened bunches, they went in. When they were all clear of the door, Albin and Derban stepped in, too, and the doors slid shut. Derban took a second to mutter secretly; "You don't have to lose your temper. You're on a hell of a thin edge this morning."

Albin flicked his eyes over the brown face, the stocky, stolid figure. "So I'm on a thin edge," he said. "Aren't you?"

"Training is training," Derban said. "Got to put up with it, because what can you do about it?"

Albin grinned wryly. "I told somebody else that, last night," he said. "Man named Dodd—hell, you know Johnny Dodd. Told him he needed some fun. Holy jumping beavers—fun."

"Maybe you need some," Derban said.

"Not like last night, I don't," Albin said, and the elevator door opened.

Now others took over, guiding the Alberts to their individual places on the training floor. Each had a small room to himself, and each room had a spy-TV high up in a corner as a safeguard.

But the spy-eyes were just as much good as the beams, Albin thought. They were useless precautions. Rebellion wasn't about to happen. It made more sense, if you thought about it, to worry the way Johnny Dodd worried, about the Confederation—against which spy-eyes and Belbis beams weren't going to do any good anyhow. (And nothing was going to happen. Nothing, he told himself firmly, was going to happen. Nothing.)

The Alberts were shunted off without trouble. Albin, heaving a small sigh, fixed the details of his next job in his mind: quality control in a smelting process. It took him a few seconds to calm down and get ready, and then he headed for room six, where one Albert waited for him, trying to think only of the job ahead, and not at all of the party, of Dr. Haenlingen, of Johnny Dodd, of rebellion and war.

He nearly succeeded.

When he opened the door the Albert inside turned, took a single look at him, and said: "I do not mean to make masters troubled."

Albin said: "What?"

"I do not ask questions now." Albin blinked, and then grinned.

"Oh," he said. "You're the one. Damn right you don't ask questions. You just listen to what I tell you—got that?"

"I listen," the Albert said.

Albin shut the door and leaned against it. "Okay," he said. "Now the first thing, you come over here and watch me." He went to the far side of the room, flicked on the remote set, and waited for it to warm up. In a few seconds it held a strong, steady picture—a single smelter, a ladle, an expanse of flooring.

"I see this when you teach me before," the Albert said in almost a disappointed tone.

"I know," Albin told it. Routine was taking over and he felt almost cheerful again. There was a woman working in the food labs in Building Two. He'd noticed her a few times in the past weeks. Now he thought of her again, happily. Maybe tonight. "This time I'm going to show you what to do," he told the Albert, and swept a hand over a row of buttons. In the smelter, metal began to heat.

The job was simple enough. The metal, once heated, had to be poured out into the ladle, which acted as a carrier to take the stuff on to its next station. The only critical point was the color of the heated liquid, and the eyes of Alberts and humans saw the same spectrum, with perhaps a little more discrimination in the eyes of the Alberts. This Albert had to be taught to let the process go unless the color was wrong, when a series of buttons would stop everything and send a quality alarm into men's quarters.

A machine could have done the job very easily, but machines were expensive. An Albert could be taught in a week.

And this one seemed to learn more quickly than most. It grasped the idea of button-pushing before the end of the day, and Albin made a mental note to see if he could speed matters up, maybe by letting the Albert have a crack at actually doing the job on its own by day four or five instead of day six.

"You learn fast," he said, when work was finally over. He felt both tired and tense, but the thought of relaxation ahead kept him nearly genial.

"I want to learn," the Albert said.

"Good boy," Albin said absently, "What's your name?"

"Cadnan."

CHAPTER SEVEN

BUT CADNAN, he knew, was only a small name. It was not a great name. He knew now that he had a great name, and it made him proud because he was no longer only small Cadnan. He was a slave.

It was good, he knew, to be a slave. A slave worked and got food and shelter from the masters, and the masters told him what he could know without even the need of asking a question. The elders were only elders, but the masters were masters, and Cadnan was a slave. It made him feel great and wise when he thought of it.

That night he could hardly wait to tell his news to Marvor—but Marvor acted as if he knew it already and was even made angry by the idea. "What is a slave?" he asked, in a flat, bad tone.

Cadnan told him of the work, the food, the shelter...

"And what is a master?" Marvor asked.

"A master is a master," Cadnan said. "A master is the one who knows."

"A master tells you what to do," Marvor said. "I am training and there is more training to come and then work. This is because of the masters."

"It is good," Cadnan said. "It is important."

Marvor shook his head, looking very much like a master himself. "What is important?" he said.

Cadnan thought for a minute. "Important is what a master needs for life," he said at last. "The masters need a slave for life, because a slave must push the buttons. Without this work the masters do not live."

"Then why do the masters not push the buttons?" Marvor

said.

"It is good they do not," Cadnan said stubbornly. "A slave is a big thing, and Cadnan is only a little thing. It is better to be big than little."

"It is better to be master than slave," Marvor said sullenly.

"But we are not masters," Cadnan said, with the air of a person trying to bring reason back to the discussion. "We do not look like masters, and we do not know what they know."

"You want to learn," Marvor said. "Then learn what they know."

"They teach me," Cadnan said. "But I am still a slave, because they teach me. I do not teach them."

Marvor hissed and at the same time shook his head like a master. The effect was not so much frightening as puzzling. He was a creature, suddenly, who belonged to both worlds, and to neither. "A master is one who does what he wants," he said. "If I do what I want, am I a master?"

"That is silliness," Cadnan said. Marvor seemed about to reply, but both were surprised instead by the opening of the door.

A master stood in the lighted entrance, holding to the sides with both hands.

Anyone with a thorough knowledge of men could have told that he was drunk. Any being with a sense of smell could have detected the odors of that drunkenness. But the Alberts knew only that a master had come to them during the time for eating and sleeping. They stirred, murmuring restlessly.

"It's all right," the master said, slurring his words only very slightly. "I wanted to come and talk. I wanted to talk to one of you."

Before anyone else could move, Cadnan was upright. "I will talk," he said in a loud voice. The others stared at him, including Marvor. Even Cadnan himself was a little surprised at his own speed and audacity.

"Come on over," the master said from the doorway. "Come on over." He made a beckoning motion.

Cadnan picked his way across the room over wakeful Alberts.

When he had reached the master, the master said: "Sit down." He looked strange, Cadnan realized, though he could not tell exactly how.

Cadnan sat and the master, closing the door, sat with his back against it. There was a second of silence, which the master broke abruptly.

"My name's Dodd," he said.

"I am called Cadnan," Cadnan said. He couldn't resist bringing out his latest bit of knowledge for display. "I am a slave."

"Sure," Dodd said dully. "I know. The rest of them say I shouldn't, but I think about you a lot. About all of you."

Cadnan, not knowing if this were good or bad, said nothing at all, but waited. Dodd sighed, shook his head and closed his eyes. After a second he went on.

"They tell me, let the slaves have their own life," he said. "But I don't see it that way. Do you see it that way? After all, you're people, aren't you? Just like us."

Cadnan tried to untangle the questions, and finally settled for a simple answer. "We are slaves," he said. "You are masters."

"Sure," Dodd said. "But I mean people. And you want the same things we do. You want a little comfort out of life, a little security—some food, say, and enough food for tomorrow. Right?"

"It is good to have," Cadnan said. He was determined to keep his end of the odd conversation up, even if it seemed to be leading nowhere.

"It isn't as if we've been here forever," Dodd said. "Only—well, a hundred or so of your years. Three generations, counting me. And here we are lording it over you, just because of an accident. We happen to be farther advanced than you, that's all."

"You are masters," Cadnan said. "You know everything."

"Not quite," Dodd said. "For instance, we don't know about you. You have—well, you have got mates, haven't you? Hell, of course you do. Male or female. Same as us. More or less."

"We have mates, when we are ready for mates," Cadnan said.

Dodd nodded precariously. "Uh-huh," he said. "Mates. They tell me I need mates, but I tried it and I got into trouble. Mates aren't the answer, kid. Cadnan. They simply aren't the answer."

Cadnan thought, suddenly, of Dara. He had not spoken to her again, but he was able to think of her. When the time of mating came, it was possible that she would be his mate...

But that was forbidden, he told himself. They came from the same tree in the same time. The rule forbade such matings.

"What we ought to do," Dodd said abruptly, "is we ought to do a thorough anthropological-anthropological study on you people. A really big job. But that's uneconomic, see? Because we know what we have to know. Where to find you, what to feed you, how to get you to work. They don't care about the rest."

"The masters are good," Cadnan said stolidly into the silence. "They let me work."

"Sure," Dodd said, and shrugged, nearly losing his balance. He recovered, and went on as if nothing at all had happened. "They let you work for them," he said. "And what do you get out of it? Food and shelter and security, I guess. But how would you like to work for yourself instead?"

Cadnan stared. "I do not understand," he said slowly.

Dodd shook his head. "No," he said. "How would you like it if there were no masters? Only people, just you and your people, living your own lives and making your own decisions? How about that, kid?"

"We would be alone," Cadnan said simply. "No master would feed us. We would die."

"No," Dodd said again. "What did you do before we came?"

"It was different," Cadnan said. "It was not good. This is better." He tried to imagine a world without masters, but the picture would not come. Obviously, then, the world he lived in was better. It was better than nothing.

"Slaves," Dodd said to himself. "With a slave mentality." And then: "Tell me, Cadnan, do they all think like you?"

Cadnan didn't think of Marvor. By now he was so confused by this strange conversation that his answer was automatic. "We do not talk about it."

Dodd looked at him mistily. "I'm disturbing you for nothing," he said. "Nothing I can do but get killed trying to start up a slave revolt. Which might be okay, but I don't know. If you get me—I don't know about that, kid. Right?" He stood up, a little shakily, still leaning against the door. "And frankly," he said, "I don't want to get killed over a lot of alligators."

"No one wishes to die," Cadnan said.

"You'd be surprised," Dodd told him. He moved and opened the door. For a second he stood in the entrance. "People can wish for almost anything," he said. "You'd be surprised." The door banged shut and he was gone.

Cadnan sat staring at the door for a second, his mind a tangle of ideas and of new words for which he had no reference whatever. When he turned away at last his eye fell on Dara, curled in a far corner. She was looking at him but when he saw her he looked away. That disturbed him, too. The rules were very clear on matings.

Cadnan wanted to tell someone what he felt. He wanted information, and he wanted someone to follow. But the masters were masters. He could not be like them. And in the room where he slept there were no elders. The thought of speaking with an elder, in any case, gave him no satisfaction. He did not want an elder. He could not join the masters and ask questions.

Somewhere, he told himself, there would be someone…

Somewhere…

Of course, there was Marvor. Later in the night, while Cadnan still lay awake trying to put thoughts and words together in his mind, Marvor moved closer to him.

"I want you with me," he said.

But Marvor, Cadnan had decided, was bad. "I sleep here," Cadnan said, a trifle severely. "I do not move my place."

In the dimness Marvor shook his head no, like a master. "I want you with me in the plan I have," he said. "I want you to help me."

That was different. The rules of the elders covered such a request. "Does a brother refuse help to a brother?" Cadnan asked. "We are from the same tree and the same time. Tell me what I must do."

Marvor opened his mouth wide, wider, until Cadnan saw the flash of his many teeth, and a second passed in silence. Then Marvor snapped his jaws shut, hissing, and spoke. "The masters tell us what to do. They make our life for us."

"This is true," Cadnan muttered.

"It is evil," Marvor said. "It is bad. We must make our own lives. Every thing makes its own life."

"We are slaves," Cadnan said. "This is our life. It is our

place."

Marvor sat up suddenly. Around them the others muttered and stirred. "Does the plant grow when a master tells it?" he asked. "Does the tree bud when a master tells it? So we must also grow in our own way."

"We are not plants or trees," Cadnan said.

"We are alive," Marvor said in a fierce, sudden whisper. "The masters, too, are alive. We are the same as they. Why do they tell us what to do?"

Cadnan was very patient. "Because they know, and we do not," he said. "Because they tell us, that is all. It is the way things are."

"I will change the way things are," Marvor said. He spoke now more softly still. "Do you want to be a master?"

"I am no master," Cadnan said wearily. "I am a slave."

"That is a bad thing." Cadnan tried to speak, but Marvor went on without stopping. "Dara is with me," he said, "and some of the others. There are not many. Most of the brothers and sisters are cowards."

Then he had to define "coward" for Cadnan—and from "coward" he progressed to another new word, "freedom." That was a big word but Cadnan approached it without fear, and without any preconception.

"It is not good to be free," he said at last, in a reasonable, weary tone. "In the cold there is a bad thing. In the rain there is a bad thing. To be free is to go to these bad things."

"To be free is to do what you want," Marvor said. "To be free is to be your own master."

After some thought Cadnan asked: "Who can be his own master? It is like being your own mate."

Marvor seemed to lose patience all at once. "Very well," he said. "But you will not tell the masters what I say?"

"Does a brother harm a brother?" Cadnan asked. That, too, was in the rules. Even Marvor, he thought sleepily, had to accept the rules.

"It is good," Marvor said equably. "Soon, very soon, I will make you free."

"I do not want to be free."

"You will want it," Marvor said. "I tell you something you do not know. Far away from here there are free ones. Ones without masters. I hear of them in the Birth Huts. They are elders who bring up their own in hiding from the masters. They want to be free."

Cadnan felt a surge of hope. Marvor might leave, take away the disturbance he always carried with him. "You will go and join them?"

"No," Marvor said. "I will go to them and bring them back and kill all the masters. I will make the masters dead."

"You cannot do it," Cadnan said instantly, shocked.

"I can," Marvor said without raising his voice. "Wait and you will see. Soon we will be free. Very soon now."

CHAPTER EIGHT

THIS IS THE END.

Dodd woke with the words in his mind, flashing on and off like a lighted sign. Back in the Confederation (he had seen pictures) there were moving stair-belts, and at the exits, at turnoffs, there were flashing signs. The words in his mind were like that. If he ignored them he would be carried on past his destination, into darkness and strangeness.

But his destination was strange, too. His head pounded, his tongue was thick and cottony in a dry mouth. Drinking had provided nothing of an escape and the price he had to pay was much too high.

This is the end.

There was no escape, he told himself dimly! The party had resulted only in that sudden appearance, the grim-mouthed old woman. Drinking had resulted in no more than this new sickness, and a cloudy memory of having talked to an Albert, some Albert, somewhere... He opened his eyes, felt pain and closed them again. There was no escape. The party Albin had taken him to had led to trouble, his own drunkenness had led to trouble. He saw the days stretching out ahead of him and making years.

It was nearly time now to begin work. To begin the job of training, with the Alberts, the job he was going to do through all those days and years lying ahead.

This is the end.

He found himself rising, dressing, shaving off the stubble of beard. His head hurt, his eyes ached, his mouth was hardly improved by a gargle, but all that was far away, as distant as his own body and his own motions.

His head turned and looked at the clock set into his wall. The eyes noted a position of the hands and passed the information to the brain: 8:47. The brain decided that it was time to go on to work. The body moved itself in accustomed patterns, opening the door, passing through the opening, shutting the door again, walking down the hallway.

All that was very distant. Dodd, himself, was— somewhere else.

He met his partner standing before a group of the Alberts. Dodd's eyes noted the expression on his partner's face. The brain registered the information, interpreted it and predicted. Dodd knew he would hear, and did hear, sounds: "What's wrong with you this morning?"

The correct response was on file. "Drinking a little too much last night, I guess." It was all automatic. Everything was automatic. The Alberts went into their elevator, and Dodd and his partner followed. Dodd's body did not stumble. But Dodd was somewhere else.

The elevator stopped, the Alberts went off to their sections, Dodd's partner went to his first assignment, Dodd found his body walking away down the hall, opening a door, going through the opening, shutting the door. The Albert inside looked up.

"Today we are going to do the work together." Dodd heard his own voice. It was all perfectly automatic, there were no mistakes. "Do you understand?"

"Understand," the Albert said.

This is the end.

At the end of the day he was back from wherever he had been, from the darkness that had wrapped his mind like cotton and removed him. There was no surprise now. There was no emotion at all: his work was over and he could be himself again. In the back of his mind the single phrase still flashed, but he had long since stopped paying attention to that.

He finished supper and went into the Commons Room, walking aimlessly.

She was sitting in a chair, with her back to the great window. As Dodd came in she looked up at him. "Hello, there."

Dodd waved a hand and, going over, found a chair and brought it to hers. "I'm sorry about the other night—"

"Think nothing of it," the girl said. "Anyhow, we're not in any trouble, and we would have been by now, if you see what I mean."

"I'm glad." He was no more than polite. There was no more in him, no emotion at all. He had reached a blank wall. There was no escape for him or for the Alberts. He could see nothing but pain ahead.

And so he had turned off the pain, and, with it, everything else.

"Do you come here often?" the girl was saying. He had been introduced to her once, but he couldn't remember her name. It was there, filed away...

"Greta Forzane," he said involuntarily.

She smiled at him, leaning a little forward. "That's right," she said. "And you're Johnny Dodd. And do you come here often?"

"...Sometimes." He waited. Soon she would stop, and he could leave, and...

And?

"Anyhow, it was just as much my fault as yours," Greta was saying. "And there's no reason why we can't be friends. All right?"

"Of course."

There was a brief silence, but he hardly noticed that.

"I'm sorry if I'm bothering you," she said.

"Not at all." His eyes were looking at her, but that made no difference. There was nothing left…nothing.

He could feel himself tighten, as if he were truly waiting for something. But there was nothing to wait for.

Was there?

"Is there something wrong?"

"Nothing. I'm fine."

"You look—"

She never finished the sentence. The storm broke instead.

Dodd found himself weeping, twisting himself in the chair; reaching out with his hands, violently racked in spasms of grief. It seemed as if the room shook and he grasped nothing until she put her hands on his shoulders. His eyes were blind with water, his body in a continual series of spasms. He heard his own voice, making sounds that had never been words, crying for—for what? Help, peace, understanding?

Somewhere his mind continued to think, but the thoughts were powerless and very small. He felt the girl's hands on his shoulders, trying to hold him, and masked by the sounds of his own weeping he heard her voice, too:

"It's all right…calm down now…you'll be all right…"

"…I…can't…" He managed to get two words out before the whirlpool sucked him down again, the reasonless, causeless whirlpool of grief and terror, his body shaking, his mouth wide open and calling in broken sounds, the tears as hot as metal marking his face as his eyes squeezed shut.

"It's all right," the voice went on saying. "It's all right."

At last he was possessed by the idea that someone else might come and see them. He drew in a breath and choked on it, and the weeping began again, but after a time he was able to take one breath and then another. He was able to stop. He reached into his pocket and found a handkerchief, wiped his eyes and looked into her face.

Nothing was there but shock, and a great caution. "What happened?" she asked. "Are you all right?"

He took a long time answering, and the answer, because it was true, surprised him. He was capable of surprise; he was capable of truth. "I don't know," he said.

PART TWO

CHAPTER NINE

"YOU WILL NOT TELL ME how to run my own division." The words were spaced, like steel rivets, evenly into the air. Dr. Haenlingen looked around the meeting-room, her face not even defiant but simply assured.

Willis, of Labor, was the first to recover. "It's not that we'd like to interfere—" he began.

She didn't let him finish. "That's a lie." Her voice was not excited. It carried the length of the room, and left no echoes.

"Now, Dr. Haenlingen—" Rogier, Metals Chairman and head of the meeting, began.

"Don't soft-soap me," the old woman snapped. "I'm too old for it and I'm too tough for it. I want to look at some facts, and I want you to look at them, too." She paused, and nobody said a word. "I want to start with a simple statement. We're in trouble."

"That's exactly the point," Willis began in his thin, high voice. "It's because we all appreciate that fact—"

"That you want to tamper," the old woman said. "Precisely." The others were seated around the long gleaming table of native wood. Dr. Haenlingen stood—her back rigid—at one end, facing them all with a cold and knowing eye. "But I won't allow tampering in my department. I can't allow it."

Rogier took a deep breath. The words came like marshmallow out of his overstuffed body. "I would hardly call a request for information 'tampering'," he said.

"I would," Dr. Haenlingen told him tartly. "I've had a very good reason, over the years, to keep information about my section in my own hands."

Rogier's voice became stern. "And that is?"

"That is," Dr. Haenlingen said, "fools like you." Rogier opened his mouth, but the old woman gave him no chance. "People who think psychology is a game, or at any rate a study that applies only to other people, never to them. People who want to subject others to the disciplines of psychology, but not themselves."

"As I understand it—" Rogier began.

"You do not understand it," the old woman said flatly. "I understand it because I have spent my life learning to do so. You have spent your life learning to understand metals, and committees. Doubtless, Dr. Rogier, you understand metals—and committees."

Her glance swept once more round the table, and she sat down. There was a second of silence before Dward, of Research, spoke up. Behind glassy contact lenses his eyes were, as always, unreadable. "Perhaps Dr. Haenlingen has a point," he said. "I know I'd hate to have to layout my work for the meeting before I had it prepared. I'm sure we can allow a reasonable time for preparation—"

"I'm afraid we can't," Rogier put in, almost apologetically.

"Of course we can't," the old woman added. "First of all, I wasn't asking for time for preparation. I was asking for noninterference. And, second, we don't have any time at all."

"Surely matters aren't that serious," Willis put in.

"Matters," the old woman said, "are a good deal more serious than that. Has anyone but me read the latest reports from the Confederation?"

"I think we all have," Rogier said calmly.

"Well, then," the old woman asked, "has anyone except

myself understood them?" The head turned, the eyes raked the table. "Dr. Willis hasn't, or he wouldn't be sounding so hopeful. The rest of you haven't, or you wouldn't be talking about time. Rogier, you haven't, or you'd quit trying to pry and begin trying to prepare."

"Preparations have begun," Rogier said. "It's just for that reason that I want to get some idea of what your division—"

"Preparations," she said. The word was like a curse. "There's been a leak, and a bad leak. We may never know where it started. A ship's officer, taking metals back, a stowaway, anything. That doesn't matter. Anyone with any sense knew there had to be a leak sooner or later."

"We've taken every possible precaution," Willis said.

"Exactly," Dr. Haenlingen told him. "And the leak happened. I take it there's no argument about that—given the figures and reports we now have?"

There was silence.

"Very well," she went on. "The Confederation is acting just as it has always been obvious they would act—with idealism, stupidity and a gross lack of what is called common sense." She paused for comment—there was none. "Disregarding the fact that they need our shipments, and need them badly, they have begun to turn against us. Against what they are pleased to call slavery."

"Well?" Rogier asked. "It is slavery, isn't it?"

"What difference do labels make?" she asked. "In any case, they have turned against us. Public opinion is swinging heavily around, and there isn't much chance of pushing it back the other way. The man in the street is used to freedom. He likes it. He thinks the Alberts ought to be free, too."

"But if they are," Willis said, "the man in the street is going to lose a lot of other things—things dependent on our shipments."

"I said they were illogical," Dr. Haenlingen told him

patiently. "Idealism almost always is. Logic has nothing to do with this—as anyone but a fool might know." She got up again, and began to walk back and forth along the end of the table. "There are still people who are convinced—I can't explain why—that minds work on logic. Minds do not work on anything resembling logic. The laws on which they do work are only now beginning to be understood and codified, but logic was thrown out the window in the days of Freud. That, gentlemen, was a long time ago. The man in the Confederation street is going to lose a lot if he insists on freeing the Alberts. He hasn't thought of that yet, and he won't think of it until after it happens." She paused, at one end of her walk, and put her hands on her hips. "That man is suffering from a disease, if putting it that way makes it easier for you to see. The disease is called idealism. Its main symptom is a disregard for consequences in favor of principles."

"But surely—" Willis began.

"Dr. Willis, you are outdoing yourself," the old woman cut in. "You sound as if you are hopeful about idealism resting somewhere even in us. And perhaps it does, perhaps it does. It is a persistent virus. But I hope we can control its more massive outbreaks, gentlemen, and not attempt to convince ourselves that this disease is actually a state of health." She began to pace again. "Idealism is a disease," she said. "In epidemic proportions, it becomes incurable."

"Then there is nothing to be done?" Dward asked.

"Dr. Rogier has his preparations," the old woman said. "I'm sure they are as efficient as they can be. They are useless, but he knows that as well as I do."

"Now wait a—" Rogier began.

"Against ships of the Confederation, armed with God alone knows what after better than one hundred years of progress? Don't be silly, Dr. Rogier. Our preparations are better than nothing, perhaps, but not much better. They can't be."

Having reached her chair again, she sat down in it. The meeting was silent for better than a minute. Dr. Rogier was the first to speak. "But, don't you see," he said, "that's just why we need to know what's going on in your division. Perhaps a weapon might be forged from the armory of psychology which—"

"Before that metaphor becomes any more mixed," Dr. Haenlingen said, "I want to clear one thing up. I am not going to divulge any basic facts about my division, now or ever."

"But—"

"I want you to listen to me carefully," she said. "The tools of psychology are both subtle and simple. Anyone can use a few of them. And anyone, in possession of only those few, will be tempted to put them to use. That use is dangerous, more dangerous than a ticking bomb. I will not run the risk of such danger."

"Surely we are all responsible men—" Rogier began.

"Given enough temptation," Dr. Haenlingen said, "there is no such thing as a responsible man. If there were, none of us would be here, on Fruyling's World. None of us would be masters, and none of the Alberts slaves."

"I'll give you an example," she said after a little time. "The Psych division has parties, parties which are rather well known among other divisions. The parties involve drinking and promiscuous sex, they get rather wild, but there is no great harm done by these activities. Indeed, they provide a useful, perhaps a necessary release." She paused. "Therefore I have forbidden them."

Willis said: "What?" The others waited.

"I have forbidden them," she said, "but I have not

stopped them. Nor will I. The fact that they are forbidden adds a certain—spice to the parties themselves. My 'discovery' of one of them does shake the participants up a trifle, but this is a minor damage. More important, it keeps alive the idea of 'forbidden fruit.' The parties are extremely popular. They are extremely useful. Were I to permit them, they would soon be neither popular nor useful."

"I'm afraid I don't quite see that," Dward put in.

Dr. Haenlingen nodded. For the first time, she put her arms on the table and leaned a little forward. "Many of the workers here," she said, "are infected by the disease of idealism. The notion of slavery bothers them. They need to rebel against the establishment in order to make that protest real to them, and in order to release hostility that might otherwise destroy us from the inside. In my own division this has been solved simply by creating a situation in which the workers fear me—fear being a compound of love, or awe, and hatred. This, however, will not do on a scale larger than one division. A dictatorship complex is set up, against which rebellion may still take place. Therefore, the parties—they serve as a harmless release for rebellious spirits. The parties are forbidden. Those who attend them are flouting authority. Their tension fades. They become good workers, for us, instead of idealistic souls, against us."

"Interesting," Rogier said. "May we take it that this is a sample of the work you have been doing?"

"You may," the old woman said flatly.

"And—about the current crisis—your suggestions—"

"My suggestion, gentlemen, is simple," Dr. Haenlingen said. "I can see nothing except an Act of God that is going to stop the current Confederation movement against us. The leak has occurred. We are done for if it affects governmental policy. My suggestion, gentlemen, is just this...pray."

Unbelievingly, Willis echoed: "Pray?"

"To whatever God you believe in, gentlemen," Dr. Haenlingen said. "To whatever God permits you to remain masters on a slave world. Pray to him—because nothing less than a God is going to stop the Confederation from attacking this planet."

PUBLIC OPINION TWO

Being an excerpt from a conversation between Mrs. Fellacia Cordon, (Citizen, white female, age thirty-eight, occupation housewife, residence 701-45 West 305 Street, New York, U. S. A., Earth) and Mrs. Gwen Brandon (Citizen, oriental female, age thirty-six, occupation housewife, residence 701-21 West 313 Street, New York, U. S. A., Earth) on a Minimart bench midway between the two homes, in the year of the Confederation two hundred and ten, on May sixteenth, afternoon.

MRS. CORDON: They've all been talking about it, how those poor things have to work and work until they drop, and they don't even get paid for it or anything.
MRS. BRANDON: What do you mean, don't get paid? Of course they get paid. You have to get paid when you work, don't you?
MRS. CORDON: Not those poor things. They're slaves.
MRS. BRANDON: Slaves? Like in the olden times?
MRS. C.: That's what they say. Everybody's talking about it.
MRS. B.: Well. Why don't they do something about it, then, the ones that are like that? I mean, there's always something you can do.
MRS. C.: They're just being forced to work until they absolutely drop, is what I hear. And all for a bunch of people who just lord it over them with guns and everything. You see, these beings—they're green, not like us, but they have feelings, too—
MRS. B.: Of course they do, Fellacia.

MRS. G.: Well. They don't have much education, hardly know anything. So when people with guns come in, you see, there just isn't anything they can do about it.

MRS. B.: Why are they let, then?

MRS. G.: Who, the people with guns? Well, nobody lets them, not just like that. It's just like we only found out about it now.

MRS. B.: I didn't hear a word on the news.

MRS. G.: You listen tonight and you'll hear a word, Gwen dear.

MRS. B.: Oh, my. That sounds like there's something up. Now, what have you been doing?

MRS. G.: Don't you think it's right, for these poor beings? I mean, no pay and nothing at all but work, work, work until they absolutely drop?

MRS. B.: What have you been doing? I mean, what can any one person do? Of course it's terrible and all that, but—

MRS. G.: We talked it over. I mean the group I belong to, you know—on Wednesday. Because all of us had heard something about it, you see, and so we brought it up and discussed it. And it's absolutely true.

MRS. B.: How can you be sure of a thing like that?

MRS. G.: We found out—

MRS. B.: When it isn't even on the news or anything.

MRS. G.: We found out that people have been talking from other places, too. Downtown and even in the suburbs.

MRS. B.: Oh. Then it must be—but what can you do, after all? It's not as if we were in the government or anything.

MRS. G.: Don't you worry about that. There's something you can do and it's not hard, either. And it has an effect. A definite effect, they say.

MRS. B.: You mean collecting money? To send them?

MRS. G.: Money won't do them any good. No. What we need is the government, to do something about this.

MRS. B.: It's easy to talk.

MRS. G.: And we can get the government to do something, too. If there are enough of us—and there will be.

MRS. B.: I should think anybody who hears about these people, Fellacia—

MRS. G.: Well, they're not people, exactly.

MRS. B.: What difference does that maker? They need help, don't they? And we can give them help. If you really have an idea?

MRS. G.: We discussed it all. And we've been writing letters.

MRS. B.: Letters? Just letters?

MRS. G.: If a Senator gets enough letters, he has to do something, doesn't he? Because the letters are from the people who vote for him, you see?

MRS. B.: But that means a lot of letters.

MRS. G.: We've had everybody sending postcards. Fifteen or twenty each. That mounts up awfully fast, Gwen dear.

MRS. B.: But just postcards—

MRS. G.: And telephone calls, where that's possible. And visits. And starting even more talk everywhere—just everywhere.

MRS. B.: Do you really think it's going to work? I mean, it seems like so little.

MRS. G.: It's going to work. It's got to.

MRS. B.: What are they working at? I mean the—the slaves.

MRS. G.: They're being forced, Gwen dear. Absolutely forced to work.

MRS. B.: Yes, dear, but what at? What do they do?

MRS. G.: I don't see where that makes any difference. Actually, nobody has been very clear on the details. But the details don't matter, do they, Gwen dear? The important thing is, we have to do something.

MRS. B.: You're right, Fellacia. And I'll—

MRS. G.: Of course I'm right.

MRS. B.: I'll start right in with the postcards. A lot of them.
MRS. G.: And don't forget to tell other people. As many as you can manage. We need all the help we can get—and so do the slaves.

CHAPTER TEN

THE DAYS PASSED and the training went on, boring and repetitious as each man tried to hammer into the obdurate head of an Albert just enough about his own particular section of machinery so that he could run it capably and call for help in case of emergencies. And, though every man on Fruyling's World disliked every moment of the job, the job was necessary, and went on. Though they, too, were slaves to a great master, none thought of rebelling. For the name of the master was necessity, and economic law, and from that rule there are no rebels. The days passed evenly and the work went slowly on.

And then the training was finished. The new Alberts went on a daily work-schedule, supervised only by the spy-sets and an occasional, deliberately random visit from a master. The visits were necessary, too. The Alberts had not the sophistication to react to a spy-set, and personal supervision was needed to convince them they were still being watched, they still had to work. A master came; a master saw them working. That, they could understand.

That—and the punishments. These went under the name of discipline, and had three grades. The Belbis beams administered all three, by means of a slight readjustment in the ray. It was angled as widely as possible, and the dispersed beam, carefully controlled, acted directly on the nervous system.

Cadnan, troubled by Marvor's threats and by his own continuing thoughts of Dara, was a trifle absent-minded and a little slower than standard. He drew punishment twice, both times in the first grade only. Albin administered both punishments, explaining to his partner Derbis that he didn't mind doing it—and, besides, someone had to.

Sometimes Dodd thought of Albin giving out discipline, and of all of his life on Fruyling's World, in terms of a sign he had once seen. It had been a joke, he remembered that clearly, but it was no more a joke now than the words that flashed nearly ignored at the back of his mind. Once or twice he had imagined this new sign hanging luridly over the entire planet, posted there in the name of profit, in the name of necessity, in the name of economic law.

EVERYTHING NOT COMPULSORY IS FORBIDDEN

The Alberts had to be trained. The Alberts had to be disciplined. The men had to work with them. The men were forbidden to leave the planet.

And who were the slaves?

That, Dodd told himself cloudily, was far from an easy decision.

Everything not compulsory was forbidden. Even the parties were forbidden...though it was always possible to find one. Dodd had avoided them completely, afraid now of another breakdown, this time in public. He had not seen Greta or called her—though he had her number now. He had stayed alone as much as possible.

He had no idea what had happened to him, and that added to his fright and to his fear of a recurrence.

But Albin, he knew, was having his fun, and so were others. The older men, it seemed, devoted themselves to running the place, to raising their families and giving good advice, to keeping production up and costs down.

The younger men had fun.

Dodd had thought of marriage. (Now, it was no more

than a memory, a hope he might once have had. Now, the end had come. There was no marriage. There was no life. Only the idea of hope remained.) He had never had the vestige of a real female image in his mind. Sometimes he had told himself to be more out-going, to meet more women— but, then, how did a man meet women?

He had fun.

And Dodd had never enjoyed that particular brand of fun—Albin's brand.

There was a Social, an acceptable party that would get him into no trouble, in Building One. Dodd felt like lying down and letting the day drain out of him into the comforting mattress there in his room. He felt like relaxing in his own company—and that, he saw suddenly, was going to mean drinking.

He could see the future unroll before him. He could see the first drink, and the tenth. Because drink was an escape, and he needed some escape from the world he was pledged to uphold, the world of slavery.

He could not afford to drink again.

So, naturally, he was getting ready to go to the Social. Albin would be there, undoubtedly, some of the older men would be there—and a scattering of women would be there, too. (He remembered himself thinking, long ago before such a party: Tonight might be the night.) He shaved very carefully, faithful to memory, dressed in the best he could find in his closet, and went out, heading for the elevator.

Tonight might be the night—but it made no difference, not any longer.

The trip to Sub-basement took a few whooshing seconds. He stepped out into a lighted, oil-smelling underground corridor, took a deep breath and headed off through gleaming passages toward another elevator at the far end. Before he reached it he took a turning, and then another.

After a magnificently confusing trip through an unmarked labyrinth, he found the elevator that led him up into the right section of Building One. That was no special feat, of course. People had been doing the like ever since the first housing-project days, on pre-Confederation Earth. Dodd never gave it a second thought. His mind was busy.

The phrase had floated to the forefront of his brain again, right behind his eyes, lighting up with a regularity that was almost soothing, almost reassuring.

This is the end.

This is the end.

This is the end.

When the elevator door slid open he was grim-faced, withdrawn, and he stepped out like a threat into a cheerful, brightly dressed crowd of people.

"Here he is!" someone shouted. "I told you he'd be here...I told you..."

Dodd turned but the words weren't meant for him. Down the corridor a knot of men and women was surrounding a new arrival from somewhere else, laughing and talking. As he stepped forward, his eyes still on that celebration, a pathway opened up for him; he was in sober black and he went through the corridor like a pencil-mark down paper, leaving an open trail as he passed.

A girl stopped him before he reached the door of the party room. She stepped directly into his path and he saw her, and his expression began to change, a little at a time, so that his eyes were, for long seconds, happier than his face, and he looked like a young bull terrier having a birthday party.

"Am I in your way?" the girl said, without budging an inch. She was dressed in a bright green material that seemed to fade so near the glowing happiness of her face. Her hair was brown, a quite ordinary brown, and even in that first second Dodd noticed her hands. They were long and slim, the thumbs pointed outward, and they were clasped at her breast in a pose that should have been mocking, but was only pleasant.

He couldn't think of anything to say. Finally he settled on: "My name's Dodd," as the simplest and quickest way of breaking the ice that surrounded him.

"Very well, then, Mr. Dodd," the girl said—she *wouldn't* go along with polite forms, "am I in your way? Because if I am, I'm terribly sorry."

"You're not in my way at all," Dodd said heavily. "I just—didn't notice you." And that was a lie, but there was nothing else to say. The thousands of words that arranged themselves so neatly into patterns when he was alone had sunk to the very bottom of his suddenly leaden mind, almost burying the flashing sign. He felt as if he were growing extra fingers and ears.

"I noticed you," the girl said. "And I said to myself, I said: 'What can a person as grim as all that be doing at a Social as gay as all this?' So I stopped you to see if I could find out."

Dodd licked his lips. "I don't know," he said. "I thought maybe I'd meet somebody. I just thought I'd like to come."

"Well," the girl said, "you've met somebody. And now what?"

Dodd found some words, not many but enough. "I haven't met you yet," he said in what he hoped was a bright tone. "What's your name?"

The girl smiled, and Dodd saw for the first time that she hadn't been smiling before. Her face, in repose, was light enough and to spare. When she smiled, he wanted smoked glasses. "Very well," she said. "My name is Fredericks. Norma Fredericks. And yours is—"

"Dodd," he said. "John Dodd. They call me Johnny."

"All right, John," she said. "You haven't been to many Socials, have you? Because I'd have seen you—I'm at everyone I can find time for. You'd be surprised how many that is. Or maybe you wouldn't."

There was no answer to the last half of that, so Dodd backtracked, feeling a shocking relief that she hadn't been to the party at which he and the other girl (whose name he could very suddenly no longer remember) had made fools of themselves. He gave her an answer to the first half of her question. "I haven't been to many Socials, no," he said. "I—" He shrugged and felt mountainous next to her. "I stay by myself, mostly," he said.

"And now you want to meet people," Norma said. "All right, Johnny Dodd—you're going to meet people!" She took him by the arm and half-led, half-dragged him to the door of the party room. Inside, the noise was like a blast of heat, and Dodd stepped involuntarily back. "Now, that's no way to be," Norma said cheerfully, and piloted him somehow inside, past a screaming crew of men and women with disposable glasses in their hands, past an oblivious couple, two couples, four, seven—past mountains and masses of color and noise and drink and singing horribly off-key, not bothersome at all, loud and raucous and somehow, Dodd thought wildly, entirely fitting. This was Norma's element, he told himself, and allowed her to escort him to a far corner of the room, where she sat him down in a chair, said: "Don't go away, don't move," and disappeared.

Dodd sat stock-still while the noise washed over him. People drifted by but nobody so much as looked in his direction, and he saw neither Albin nor that other forgettable girl, for all of which he was profoundly grateful. He hadn't been to a Social since his last mistake, and before that it had been almost two years, he realized with wonder. He'd forgotten just how much of everything it could be. He devoted a couple of minutes to catching his breath, and then he just watched people, drifting, standing, forming new combinations every second. He thought (once) he saw Albin in the middle of a crowd near the door, but he told himself he was probably mistaken. There was no one else he recognized. He didn't grow tired, but sitting and watching, he found, was exhilarating enough.

In another minute, he was sure Norma wasn't going to come back. Probably she had found someone else, he told himself in what he thought was a reasonable manner. After all, he wasn't a very exciting person. She had probably started off to get him a drink or something, with the best of intentions, and met someone more interesting on the way.

He had just decided that, after all, he couldn't really blame her, when she appeared at his side.

"The punch," she announced, "is authentic. It is totally authentic. One glass and you forget everything. Two, and you remember. Three—I don't know what happens with the third glass yet. But I'm going to find out."

He looked at her hands. She was holding two disposable glasses, full of purple liquid. He took one from her and got up. "Well," he said, "cheers."

"Also down the hatch," she said. "And any other last year's slang you happen to have around and want to get rid of." She lifted the glass. "Here's to you, John Dodd," she said, and tipped the glass at her lips—just that. He had never before seen anyone drink in just that way, or drink so quickly. In seconds, before he had taken a sip (he was so amazed, watching her), the glass was empty. "Whoosh," she said clearly. "That ought to hold me for at least six minutes."

Then she noticed that he hadn't started his own drink yet, so he took a cautious sip. It tasted like grape juice, like wine, like—he couldn't identify the ingredients, and besides he was watching her face. He took another sip.

"That's the way," Norma approved. "Soon you'll be drinking with the big boys."

And whether she was making fun of him or not hardly mattered. He felt careless. Maybe the drink had done it. "Why did you pick me?" he heard himself say. "Why did you stop me, out of all those people?"

She hesitated, and when she spoke it sounded like the truth, perhaps too much like the truth to be true. "You looked like a puppy," she said seriously. "Like a puppy trying to act fierce. Maybe I've always had a weakness for dumb animals. No offense meant, John Dodd."

The idea of being offended hadn't occurred to him, but he tried it out experimentally and discovered he didn't like it. Before he could say anything, though, Norma had become energetic again.

"Enough analysis," she said abruptly, so strongly that he wasn't sure what she meant by the words. "Sit down—sit down." He felt for the chair behind him and sat. Norma cast a keen eye over the nearby crowds, spotted an empty chair and went off for it. "Later," she told him, when she had placed herself next to him, "we can join the crowd. For now, let's get—let's get better acquainted, Johnny."

"That's the first time you've called me Johnny," he said.

"So it is," she said. Her face was a mask, and then it lightened. "What do you work at, Johnny?"

"I'm in Building Three," he said. It was easier to answer her than anatomize the confusions he felt. "I work with smelting and quality control—you know." He took another sip of his drink, and found to his surprise that it was more than half-gone.

"With the Alberts," she said. "I know."

He thought he read her look correctly. "I don't like it either," he told her earnestly. "But somebody has to do it. I think—"

"You don't have to get defensive," Norma said. "Relax. Enjoy yourself. Join the party. Did I look at you as if you were a murderer of small children?"

"I just—don't like it," he said carefully. "I—well, there isn't anything I can do about it, is there?"

"I wouldn't know," she said, and then (had she made a decision? He couldn't tell) she went on: "I'm in Psych, myself."

"Psych? You?"

"Psych, me," she said. "So I'm every bit as responsible as you are. And maybe the reason there's nothing to do is—is because it's already been done."

"Already been done?" Dodd swallowed the rest of his drink in one gulp and leaned toward her. Norma looked down at her own empty glass.

"There are rumors," she said. "Frankly, I'd rather they didn't get around. And if I hadn't had too much to drink— or something—I wouldn't even be mentioning them. I'm sorry."

"No," he said, surprising himself. "Tell me. What rumors?"

Norma kept her eyes on her glass. "Nothing," she said, in a new, strained voice.

Dodd remained in the same position, feeling more tense than he could ever remember having felt. "Tell me," he said. "Come on. If you've gone this far—"

"I suppose I have," she said. "I suppose I've gone too far now, haven't I?"

"You've got to tell me."

"Yes," she said. "It's—they say the Confederation knows. I mean knows what we're doing here. Officially. Everything." She dropped the glass then and Dodd stooped ridiculously to pick it up. It lay between their chairs. He felt the blood rushing to his head. There was pounding in his temples. He got the glass and gave it to her but she took it absently, as if she hardly noticed him. "Of course, it's just a rumor," she said in a low voice.

"The people know," Dodd said. "It's out. It's all out. About the slavery. Is that what you mean?"

She nodded. "I'm sorry."

"But it's important—" he began, and stopped. He looked at his glass, still empty. He took a breath, began again. "I work with them. I'm part of it. It's important to me."

"Just as important to me," Norma said. "Believe me, Johnny. I'm responsible, too."

"But you're in Psych," he said. "That's—morale. Nothing more than morale, as far as I know—"

She raised her head and looked him full in the face, her eyes like a bright challenge. Her face was quite sober when she spoke. "I'm in Psych, but it's more than morale, Johnny. We're—always thinking up new ways to keep the little Alberts in their place. Put it that way. Though nobody's really come up with an improvement on the original notion."

"The original notion?"

Now her smile gave light and no heat, a freak of nature. "The original specific," she said. She paused for a second and the mockery in her voice grew more broad. "That old-time religion," she said, drawing the words out like fine, hot wire. "That old-time religion, Johnny Dodd."

CHAPTER ELEVEN

THE WORK WENT ON, for Cadnan as well as for the masters. Days passed and he began to improve slightly. He received no further discipline, and he was beginning to settle into a routine. Only thoughts of Dara disturbed him—those, and the presence of Marvor, who was still apparently waiting to make good his incomprehensible threat.

Marvor had said he was going to leave, but he still appeared every evening in the same room. Cadnan had hardly dared to question him, for fear of being drawn into the plan, whatever it was. He could only wait and watch and wish for someone to talk to. But, of course, there was no one.

And then, one day during the first part of his working shift, a master came into the room, the very master who had gone with Cadnan through his training. "You're Cadnan?" he asked.

Cadnan said: "I am Cadnan."

The master beckoned through the open door of Cadnan's working-room, and two more masters appeared, strange ones, leading between them an elder. The elder, Cadnan saw at once, had lived through many matings. The green skin of his arms was turning to silver, and his eye was no longer bright, but dulling fast with age. He looked at the working-room and at the young Albert with blank caution.

"This one is called Gornom," the master said. "He'll be with you when you work. He's going to help you work—you can teach him all he has to know. Just make sure you don't let him handle the buttons until we give you the word. All right?"

Cadnan understood. "All right," he said, and the three masters left the room without more words. The door shut behind them and Gornom visibly relaxed. Yet there was still wariness behind the old eye. "I work in the field," he said after a second. "I am good worker in the field."

Cadnan knew from gossip about the field. That was the place where the metal lay. Alberts worked there, digging it up and bringing it to the buildings where Cadnan and many like him took over the job. He nodded slowly, bending his body from the waist instead of from the neck like the masters, or Marvor. "If you are in the field," he said, "why do you come here? This is not a place for diggers."

"I am brought here," Gornom said. "I am an elder many times. What the masters say, I do. Now they say I come here, and I come."

Cadnan looked doubtful. "You are to work with me?"

"So the masters say." That was unanswerable, and Cadnan accepted it. He flicked a glance at the TV screen, which showed him the smelting process, and leaped for the buttons. After a few minutes of action he was finished. There was a slight breathing space.

"I am to tell you what to do," he said.

Gornom looked grave. "I see what it is you do," he said. "It is a lesson. When you act for the masters, the great machines obey you."

"It is true," Cadnan said.

"This is the lesson," Gornom said slowly, as if it were truly important. "We are shown the machines so that we may learn to be like the machines. When the master tells us what to do, we are to do it. There is nothing else."

Cadnan thought about that. It made sense. It made a structure he could understand, and it made the world a less confusing place. "You have said a truth," he judged at last.

"It is one of many truths," Gornom said. And that was an invitation, Cadnan recognized. He hesitated no more than a second.

"Where may I learn the others?" But Gornom didn't answer, and Cadnan's breathing space was over. He had to be back at the board, pushing buttons, watching carefully, Gornom stood behind him, peering over his shoulder with a cloudy eye. Neither said a word until the new spell of work was over. Then Cadnan repeated his question.

"It is not for all," Gornom said distantly. "One must be chosen."

"You have come to me," Cadnan said. "You have been sent to me. Is this what you call chosen?"

It was the right answer, perhaps the only right answer. Gornom pretended to consider the matter for a minute, but his mind was already made up. "We are above you, on the floor over yours," he said. "When our work is finished I will take you there."

Cadnan imagined a parade of new truths, a store of knowledge that would lay all his questions to rest and leave him, as after a meal, entirely satisfied. He went back to work and contemplated the first of the truths. He was to be like the machine. He promised himself he would try to imitate the machine, doing only what the masters ordered. And for the rest of that day, indeed, life seemed to make perfect calming sense.

But, after all, Gornom was only an elder and not a master. He could be wrong.

The doubt appeared at the end of the day, but by then Gornom had the younger Albert in tow. They took the elevator up one flight and went to Gornom's room. The novelty of all of this excited Cadnan so that he nearly forgot his new doubts. They shrank perceptibly without disappearing altogether.

Gornom opened the door of the new room. Inside, Cadnan saw six elders, sitting in a circle on the floor. The circle, incomplete, was open toward the door, and all six big eyes were staring at the newcomers. The floor was nearly bare. The leaves had been brushed into mounds that lay in the corners.

Without a word, Gornom sat in the circle and motioned Cadnan to a place beside him. Moving slowly and uncertainly, Cadnan came forward and sat down. There was a second of absolute silence.

One of the other elders said: "You bring a new one to us?"

"I bring a new one," Gornom said.

The other elder, leaning forward from the waist, peered at Cadnan. His eye was larger than normal, and glittering cold. He, like many of the highest elders, looked somewhat humanoid, unlike most slaves. Cadnan, awestruck, neither spoke nor moved, and the elder regarded him for a time and then said abruptly: "Not all are called to the truth."

"He has been called," Gornom said. "He has been chosen."

"How is he chosen?"

Gornom explained. When he had finished, a silence thick as velvet descended upon the room. Then, very suddenly, all the elders spoke at once.

"May the masters live forever."

Cadnan, by this time, was nearly paralyzed with fright. He sat very still. The elders continued, in a slow, leaden chorus:

"May the masters live forever.

"May the words live forever.

"May the lessons live forever.

"May the truths live forever."

Then the velvet silence came down again, but the words

rang through it faintly until Gornom broke the spell with speech.

"The young one has come to learn. He has come to know the truths." He looked around at the others and then went on: "His name is Cadnan. He wishes to have your names. Let him have your names."

The elder who had spoken first identified himself as Lonak. The others gave their names in order: Dalor, Puna, Grudoc, Burlog, and Montun. Cadnan stared with fascinated eyes at Puna, who was older than anyone he had ever seen. His skin was nearly all white, and in the dim room it seemed to have a faint shine. His voice was very high and thin, like a wind sighing in tall tree-branches. Cadnan shivered, but didn't take his eye from Puna until, as if at a signal, all the elders rose. Awkwardly, then, Cadnan rose with them, again confused and still frightened.

He saw Gornom raise his hands over his head and chant: "Tall are the masters."

All the others repeated the words.

"Wise are the masters."

Cadnan, this time, repeated the phrase with the elders.

"Good are the masters."

When the antiphon had been delivered Gornom waited a full second and then fell prostrate to the floor. The others followed his example, except for Cadnan, who, afraid to let himself fall on bare metal, crouched down slowly instead.

"Weak are the slaves," Gornom whispered.

The answer was a whisper, too.

"Small are the slaves."

The others whispered.

"They are like small ones all the days of their lives, and only the masters are elders."

"The masters are elders."

"As the machine obeys," Gornom said, "so the slave

obeys. As the tree obeys, so the slave obeys. As the metal obeys, so the slave obeys. As the ground obeys, so the slave obeys."

"So the slave obeys."

Then there was silence again, not as profound as before. Through it, Cadnan could hear the others whispering, but he couldn't quite catch their words. He was later told what praying was, though he never had a chance to practice it.

And then everyone returned to the original circle, and squatted. In what was almost a normal tone Gornom said: "Here is our new one. He must be told."

Puna himself rose. "I will tell him." And Cadnan, frightened by the very look of the elder, could do nothing but follow him as he beckoned and went to a corner near a mound of leaves. The others, scattered, were eating. Cadnan picked up a leaf, but Puna took it gently out of his hand.

"We do not eat until it is over," he said quietly.

Cadnan accepted this without words, and Puna told him the legend. During the entire tale, Cadnan, stock-still, didn't even think of interrupting. At first his attention wandered to the leaves, but as Puna's voice went on he listened more and more closely, and even his fright began to leave him under the legend's fascination.

"Long ago, the masters come to the world, sent by the Great Elder. We are no more than children. We do not work, we do nothing except eat and sleep and live out our lives in the world. The Great Elder makes us the gift of talking and the gift of trees, and he makes the rules of the trees.

"Then he does nothing more for us. First we must become more than children, more than small ones.

"For this he sends the masters.

"The masters are good because they show us work and

give us machines that have power. Our power is over the masters because of the machines. But we may not use such power. They are elder to us. They are wiser than we are. Only when we become so wise we use power against them, and in that day master and slave are one. In that day the Great Elder returns to his small ones.

"In this time there is the work, and the work makes us always more like the masters. We live in the buildings like masters. We work with machines like masters. We do what the masters say. Soon we are all the same.

"No one can tell when we are like masters in all things. We know of it when the Great Elder returns to us. All must watch and wait for that day. In this time, we only remember and tell ourselves the truths over and over. There are many truths and some I can not speak. Here are the others:

"The masters are our elders.

"The machines are under obedience to us while we obey the masters.

"The Great Elder wishes our obedience to the masters.

"If we disobey the masters the machines and the trees will not obey us, and there will be no more work and no small ones. For this is the order of the world—some obeying and some to be obeyed. It is visible and plain. When the chain is broken all the chain breaks."

Puna paused, and then repeated the last sentence.

"When the chain is broken all the chain breaks."

"It is true," Cadnan said excitedly. "It is true. Yet there is more truth—"

"There is," Puna said soberly. "We meet again in five days' time. I can count five days, and so the others will know, and you will know. At this next meeting you will be told more truths." His smile was thin and distant. "Now eat."

Cadnan reached numbly for a leaf and, without thinking, began to nibble. The world had been set in order. He had no more questions now. Instead, he felt empty spaces, waiting to be filled with the great knowledge of Puna and of Gornom and all the others, at the next meeting.

And at other meetings, after that...

He put that thought away. It was too much and too large. The one certain thing was that in five days' time (whenever that was) he would know more. In five days they would all meet again.

He hoped five days was not too long.

As matters turned out, of course, he need not have worried. The meeting he was waiting for never happened.

And, after that, there were no more meetings at all.

PUBLIC OPINION THREE

Being excerpts from memo directives sent between executives of Associated Metallic Products, Ltd., a corporation having its main offices within Dome Two, Luna City, Luna, and associated offices on all three inhabited planets, the memo directives being dated between May fourteenth and May twenty-first, in the Year of the Confederation two hundred and ten.

TO: John Harrison
FROM: Fredk. Ramsbotham
RE: Metals supplies & shipment

It having come to my attention that the process of metals shipment is in danger because of a threat to the materials and procurement divisions of AMP, Ltd., I wish to advise you, as current Chairman of the Board, of the nature of the emergency, and request your aid in drawing up plans to deal with it.

According to reports from our outside operatives, and such statistical checking as we have been able to use in a matter of this nature, there exists a strong possibility that present procurement procedures regarding our raw materials may at any moment be abrogated by act of the Confederation government. The original motive for this action would seem to be a rising tide of public unrest, sparked apparently by chance disclosure of our procurement procedures. That the public unrest may very soon reach the point at which Confederation notice, and hence Confederation action, may be taken is the best judgment both of our outside operatives and of our statistical department.

In order to deal with this unprecedented emergency, it would be advisable to have your thoughts on the matter. With these in hand...

TO: Fred Ramsbotham
FROM: John Harrison
RE: Your memo May 14

My God, Fred, I haven't seen such a collection of verbiage since Latin class. Why not say what you mean? People are calling the setup on Fruyling's World slavery, and slavery is a nasty word.

Let's get together for a talk—and what's with the high-sounding guff? You sound sore about something. What?

TO: James Oliver Gogarty
FROM: Leonard Offutt
RE: Statistical findings

...The situation is serious, J. O., and there's no getting around it. If the Government has to take action there's only one way (given current majorities) they're going to be able to move, and that's to declare Fruyling's World a protectorate, or some such (get your lawyers to straighten out the terminology—in plain and simple English, a ward of the state), and "administer" the place for the best interests of the natives.

Get that—the natives.

Never mind us, never mind AMP, never mind the metals we need.

No, the Government will step in and take all that away from us in the interests of a bunch of silly green-looking monsters who can barely talk and can't, as near as I can see, think at all.

Statistics doesn't give us much of a chance of heading them off. As a matter of fact, any recommended course of action has better than a 50% chance of making matters even worse. And if you don't think they can be worse, take a look at the attached sheet, which...

TO: John Harrison
FROM: Fredk. Ramsbotham
RE: Your memo May 15

Have you never heard of the Confederation impounding records? Or these memos, for instance?

TO: Fred Ramsbotham
FROM: John Harrison
RE: Your memo May 15

Have you never heard of AMP burning them, you silly damn fool?

Now let's get together for a talk.

TO: James Oliver Gogarty
FROM: Gregory Whiting and staff
RE: Your memo May 17

Pressure put on Confederation executives and members of the Senate might convince the Confederation that, without a fight, Fruyling's World would not surrender to Confederation control.

It might not be advisable to begin such a fight. Even with

modern methods of transport and training, the weapons gap between the Confederation and Fruyling's World is a severe handicap. In other words, J. O., if it came to a showdown the people here don't think we stand a fair chance of coming out on top.

You'd better rethink your position, then…

TO: James Oliver Gogarty
FROM: John Harrison
RE: Fruyling's World

Interoffice guff says you're planning definite moves on your own, J. O., and against some opposition. I'm still Chairman of the Board around here, and I intend to use power if I have to. The best advice I can get tells me your plans are unadvisable.

Get it through your head that this has nothing to do with the Board elections. This is a serious matter. I can stop you, J. O., and don't think I won't if it comes to that. But I don't want to make threats.

There must be something we can do—but we're going to have to devote more thought to the whole matter first.

TO: James Oliver Gogarty
FROM: Leonard Offutt
RE: Statistical findings

Chances of such pressure succeeding are, according to derived figures, 37%. Chances of the pressure leading to actual attack on Fruyling's World (see attached sheet) are 58%.

We cannot advise…

TO: Fredk. Ramsbotham
FROM: James Oliver Gogarty
RE: Attached statistical findings

...Of course it's a risk, Frederick, but we're in the risk-taking business, and we always were, as your father used to say, and mine too. Between us, John is a cautious old man, and the rest of the Board is beginning to appreciate that. By next year the entire situation may have changed.

I'm asking for your support, then, as a matter of practical politics. In a risky matter like this one, support can make all the difference between...

TO: James Oliver Gogarty
FROM: John Harrison
RE: My memo May 19
     J. O., I mean it.
     Now layoff.

TO: Williston Reed
FROM: John Harrison
RE: Current memo series

As you know, I'm keeping you up to date whenever I have a minute between appointments. A publicity chief ought to know everything, inside as well as public-issue material, if only so he can be conscious of what to hide. I've tried to work with you as well as I can, and if there are delays in reporting, you'll understand that pressure of other duties...

...The story behind all of this is simple enough. The takeover Gogarty and Ramsbotham have been trying to pull is interfering with practical business. Frankly, AMP's competitors are happy enough to jump in and stir the pot. I think they've been buying up Senators here and there (for which there is enough precedent; the entire Senate hasn't been bought since the Dedrick mutiny forty years back but you don't need the entire Senate if you have a few key men, and I've always thought Dedrick's lawyers were wasteful), and beyond what the competition's been active in, there are always the fanatics. Freedom for all—you know the sort of thing.

Now the big danger is that if R. and G. succeed in keeping things messed up the rest of the metals boys will step in, push the government into the right moves, and kill Fruyling's World deader than Dedrick himself. Which (according to the statistical breakdown) won't put us into the bankruptcy courts, but will slide us from a first-or-second spot to a ninth-or-tenth one. The big question is whether you'd rather be a small frog in a big puddle or the reverse. Me, I'd rather be a big frog in a big puddle than any other combination I can think of, and in spite of everything I think I'm going to go on being just that.

Fruyling's World has been around for a long time, but the current AMP fight gives the competition the opportunity they need, and they're pushing it. If we can weather the storm...

Well, I'm being gloomy. Of course we can weather the storm. I'll swing Gogarty back, and that will leave Ramsbotham nowhere to go...

TO: John Harrison
FROM: Fredk. Ramsbotham
RE: Fruyling's World

...Support of the suggestion put forward by Mr. Gogarty at the last Board meeting was not, believe me, given without grave consideration.

Now that the matter has been decided, I hope we can all pull together like team-mates, and "let the dead past bury its dead." I'm sure that...

TO: Fred Ramsbotham
FROM: John Harrison
RE: Your memo May 21

I'm worrying a little more about burying some of the currently living—our own men on Fruyling's World.

I've got to ask you to reconsider...

TO: All news services, for immediate release
FROM: Williston Reed

As almost his first act on taking his position as Chairman of the Board of Associated Metallic Products, Ltd., Frederick Ramsbotham today issued a statement of policy regarding "interference by Confederation governmental officials" in what he termed the "private business of AMP."

Mr. Ramsbotham, whose recent election came as a surprise to many shareholders, has stated his intention of "remaining firm in continuance of present policies" regardless of what he described as "threats" from Confederation officials.

He states that his duty to shareholders of AMP must include protection of the private and profit-making enterprise being carried on at Fruyling's World, and that such private concerns are not "the business of public government."

As former Chairman of the Board, John Harrison was asked to comment on the position taken by Mr. Ramsbotham. Mr. Harrison stated that he disagreed with the particular stand taken by Mr. Ramsbotham in this matter, but sympathized with his strong feelings of duty toward the shareholders of the concern.

Confederation response was reported to be "immediate and strong" by sources high in the government, but as yet no final word has been received regarding what action, if any, is contemplated...

TO: Fredk. Ramsbotham
FROM: John Harrison
SUBJECT: The daily paper

Now you've torn it.

Unless you think we can make money selling weapons to be used against our own people on Fruyling's World.

I've sold out my shares as of this morning, Fred. I'm through. I think you are, too—whether you know it or not just yet.

CHAPTER TWELVE

"THAT OLD-TIME religion."

Dodd heard the words echoing in his mind that night, and the next night, and the next. All that she had said:

"We set up a nice pie-in-the-sky sort of thing, all according to the best theory, just the thing to keep the Alberts happy and satisfied and working hard for us. It started right after the first setup here, and by now I guess the Alberts think they invented it all by themselves, or their Great Elder came down from a tree and told them."

"It's horrible," he had said.

"Of course it is." There was a silence. "But you said it yourself...what can we do? We're here and we're stuck here."

"But—"

Norma hadn't wanted to argue, but the argument went on in Dodd's mind, and it still continued, circling in his mind like a buzzard. There was nothing he could do about it, nothing Norma could do about it. He avoided even the thought of seeing her for a few days, and then he found himself making an excuse to go over to Building One. While walking to the building, Dodd noticed a group of three Elders dressed in green attire with leafy crowns engaged in prayers to a deity that didn't even exist. Minutes later he met Norma.

And what she had disclosed to him, what they spoke of, made no difference that he could see in what he felt.

He was happy. Slowly he realized that he had hardly ever been happy before.

He even forgot, for a time, about the rumors, the threat of

Confederation troops that had hung over her words like a gray cloud. All he could think of was Norma, and the terrible thing in which they were both bound up.

He told himself grimly that it would never have bothered Albin, for instance. Albin would have had his fun with Norma, and that would have been that.

But it bothered Johnny Dodd.

He was still worrying over it, and in spite of himself finding happiness, when the escape came, and the end.

CHAPTER THIRTEEN

"THERE'S NOTHING to be done about it." Dr. Haenlingen delivered the words and sat down rigidly behind her desk. Norma nodded, very slowly.

"I know that," she said. "I started out—I started to do just what you wanted. To talk to him, draw him out, find out just what he did feel and what he planned."

"And then something happened," Dr. Haenlingen said tightly. "I know."

Norma paced to the window and looked out, but the day was gray. She saw only her own reflection. "Something happened," she murmured, "I—guess I had too much to drink. I wanted to talk."

"So I understand," Dr. Haenlingen said. "And you talked. And—whatever his situation—you managed to increase his tension rather than understand or lessen it."

Norma shook her head at the reflection. "I'm sorry."

"I have often found," Dr. Haenlingen said, "that sorrow following an action is worse than useless. It usually implies a request to commit the same action again."

"But I wouldn't—" Norma said, turning, and then stopped before the calm gaze of the old woman.

"No?" Dr. Haenlingen said.

"I'll try to—"

Dr. Haenlingen lifted a hand and brushed the words aside. "It doesn't matter," she said. "I am beginning to see that it doesn't matter."

"But—"

"All we can do now is wait," Dr. Haenlingen said. "We

are—outplayed."

There was a little silence. Norma waited through it without moving.

"Would you like to have a lesson in psychology?" Dr. Haenlingen said in the graying room. "Would you like to learn a little, just a little, about your fellow man?"

Norma felt suddenly frightened. "What's wrong?"

"Nothing is wrong," Dr. Haenlingen said. "Everything is moving along exactly as might have been predicted. If we had known what the Confederation planned, and exactly the timetable of their actions...but we did not, and could not. Norma, listen to me."

The story she told was very simple. It took a fairly long time to tell.

Slavery takes a toll of the slaves (as the Confederation was beginning to find out, as the idealists, the do-gooders, were beginning, however slowly to realize). But it takes a toll of the masters, too.

The masters can't quite rid themselves of the idea that beings which react so much like people may really (in spite of everything, in spite of appearance, in spite of laws and regulations and social practices) be people, after all, in everything but name and training.

And it just wouldn't be right to treat people that way...

Slaves feel pain. In simple reciprocity, masters feel guilt.

And because (according to the society, and the laws, and the appearances, and the regulations) there was no need for guilt, the masters of Fruyling's World had, like masters anywhere and any time, buried the guilt, hidden it even from themselves, forbidden its existence and forgotten to mention it to their thoughts.

But the guilt remained, and the guilt demanded.

Punishment was needed.

"They're going to fight," Dr. Haenlingen said. "When the Confederation attacks, they're going to fight back. It's senseless. Even if we won, the Confederation fleet could blockade us, prevent us getting a shipment out, bottle us up and starve us for good. But they don't need sense, they need motive, which is quite a different thing. They're going to fight—both because they need the punishment of a really good licking, and because fighting is one more way for them to deny their guilt."

"It seems complex," Norma said.

"Everything is complex," Dr. Haenlingen said, "as soon as human beings engage in it. The action is simple enough: warfare."

"We've got to stop them—"

Dr. Haenlingen went on as if she hadn't heard. "The action serves two different, indeed two contradictory purposes. If you think that's something rare in the actions of mankind, you must be more naive than you have any right to be."

"We've got to stop them," Norma said again. "Got to. They'll die—we'll all die."

"There is nothing to do," Dr. Haenlingen said. "We are outplayed—by the Confederation, by our own selves. We are outplayed. There are no moves left. There is nothing I can offer, nothing anyone can offer, quite as attractive as the double gift of punishment and denial." Shockingly, for the first time, the old woman sounded tired. Her voice was thin in the gray room. "Nothing we can do, Norma. You're dismissed. Go back to work."

"But you can't just give up—you can show them there aren't any real reasons, show them they're not being rational—"

"Oh, but they'll be rational," Dr. Haenlingen said in the same still voice. "Wait for the rumors to start, Norma. Wait

166

for them to begin telling each other that the Confederation is going to kill them all anyhow, take them back and hang them as war criminals—"

"That's ridiculous!"

"Perhaps."

"Then—"

"Rumors during a war are almost always ridiculous. That fact makes no difference at all. They'll be believed—because they have to be believed."

Norma thought. "We can start counter-rumors."

"Which would not be believed. They offer nothing, nothing that these people want. Oh, yes, people can be changed—" Dr. Haenlingen paused. "Given sufficient time and sufficient equipment, it is possible to make anyone into anything, anything at all. But to change these people, to make them act as we want—the time required is more than ten years, Norma. And we haven't got ten years."

"We've got to try," Norma said earnestly.

"What we have got," Dr. Haenlingen said, "is more like ten days. And there is nothing to do in ten days. The people have spoken. Vox populi…" The eyes closed. There was a silence. Norma waited, astonished, horrified. "Perhaps it is necessary," Dr. Haenlingen's voice said. "Perhaps…we must wait. *Ich kann nicht anders…*"

"What?" Norma asked.

"Martin Luther," Dr. Haenlingen's voice said, remote and thin. "It means: 'I can do nothing else.' He wrote it as his justification for a course of action that was going to get him excommunicated, perhaps killed."

"But—"

Dr. Haenlingen said nothing, did nothing. The body sat behind its desk in the gray room. Norma stared, then turned and fled.

CHAPTER FOURTEEN

THE MIXTURE OF FEELINGS inside Cadnan was entirely new to him, and he couldn't control it very well. He found himself shaking without meaning to, and was unable to stop himself. There was relief, first of all, that it was all over, that he no longer had to worry about what Marvor might have planned, or whether Marvor were going to involve him. There was fright, seeing anyone carry through such a foolhardy, almost impious idea in the teeth of the masters. And there was simple disappointment, the disappointment of a novice theologue who has seen his pet heretic slip the net and go free.

For Cadnan had tried, earnestly, night after night, to convert Marvor to the new truths the elders had shown him. They were luminously obvious to Cadnan, and they set the world in beautiful order; but, somehow, he couldn't get through to Marvor at all, couldn't express the ideas he had well enough or convincingly enough to let Marvor see how beautiful and true all of them really were. For a time, in fact, he told himself with bitterness that Marvor's escape had really been all his own fault. If he'd only had more talks with Marvor, he thought cloudily, or if he'd only been able to speak more convincingly...

But regret is part of a subjunctive vocabulary. At least one writer has noted that the subjunctive is the mark of civilization. This may be true—it seems true. In Cadnan's case, at any rate, it certainly was true. Uncivilized, he spent little time in subjunctive moods. All that he had done, all that Marvor had done, was open to him, and he remembered it often—but, once the bad first minutes were past, he remembered everything with less and less regret. The mixture, as it stood, was heady enough for Cadnan's untrained emotions.

He had tried to talk to Marvor about the truths, of course. Marvor, though, had been obstinately indifferent. Nothing made any impression on his hardened, stubborn mind. And now he was gone.

Dara had the news first. She came into their common room at the end of the day, very excited, her hands still moving as if she were turning handles in the refinery even after the close of work. Cadnan, still feeling an attraction for her, and perceiving now that something had disturbed her, stayed where he was squatting. Attraction for Dara, and help given to her, might lead to mating, and mating was against the rule. But Dara came to him.

"Do you know what happens with Marvor?" she said. Her voice, always quiet, was still as sweet to Cadnan as it had ever been. "He is gone, and the masters do not know where."

The mixture of emotions began—surprise and relief first, then regret and disappointment, then fear, all boiling and bubbling inside him like a witches' stew. He spoke without thinking: "He is gone to break the chain of obedience. He is gone to find others who think as he thinks."

"He is escaped," Dara said. "It is the word the masters use, when they speak of this."

"It happens before now," Cadnan told her. "There are others, whom he joins."

Dara shut her eye. 'It is true. But I know what happens when there is an escape. In the place where my work is, there is one from Great Bend Tree. She tells me of what happens."

Dara fell silent and Cadnan watched her nervously. But he had no chance to speak. She began again, convulsively.

"When this other escapes it is from a room of Great Bend Tree." Cadnan nodded. He and Dara were of Bent Line Tree, and hence in a different room. The segregation, simple for the masters, was handy and unimportant, and so it was used. Cadnan thought it natural. Every tree had its own room.

"Do they find the one who escapes?" he asked.

"They find him. The masters come in and they punish the others from the room."

Precedent was clearly recognizable, even though it made no sense. Those who had not escaped surely had no reason to be punished, Cadnan thought. But what the masters had done to Great Bend Tree they would do to Bent Line Tree.

Everyone would be punished.

With a shock he realized that "everyone" included Dara.

He heard himself speak. "You must go."

Dara looked at him innocently. "Go?" she asked.

"You must go as Marvor has gone. The masters do not take you for punishment if you go."

"There is nothing for me to do," she said, and her eye closed. "No. I wait for you, but only to tell you this…there is nothing I can do."

"Marvor is gone," Cadnan said slowly. "You, too, can go. Maybe the masters do not find you. If you stay you are punished. If you go and they do not find you there is no punishment for you." It amazed him that she could not see so clear a point.

"Then all can go," she said. "All can escape punishment."

Cadnan grunted, thinking that over. "Where one goes," he said at last, "one can go. Maybe many cannot go."

Her answer was swift. "And you?"

"I stay here," he said, trying to sound as decisive as possible.

Dara turned away. "I do not listen to your words," she

said flatly. "I do not hear you or see you."

Cadnan hissed in anguish. She had to understand...
"What do I say that is wrong? You must—"

"You speak of my going alone," she said. "But that is me,
and no more. What of the others?'"

"Marvor," Cadnan said after a second. "He is to come
and aid them. He tells me this. We join him and come back
with him, away from here, to where he stays now. Then none
of us are punished." He paused. "It will be a great
punishment."

"I know," Dara said. "Yet one does not go alone."

Her voice was so low that Cadnan could barely hear it, but
the words were like sharp stones, stabbing fear into his body.
For the first time, he saw clearly exactly what she was driving
at. And after a long pause, she spoke again.

'Where one goes, two may go. Where Marvor goes, two
may follow, one to lead the other."

"One goes alone," Cadnan said, feeling himself tremble
and trying to control it. "You must go."

It seemed a long time before she spoke again, and Cadnan
held himself tightly, until his muscles began to ache.

"We go together," she said at last. "Two go where one
has gone. Only so do I leave at all."

It was an ultimatum, and Cadnan understood what was
behind it. But an attraction between Dara and himself... He
said, "There is the rule of the tree," but it was like casting
water on steel.

"If we leave here," Dara said, "why think of a smaller
rule?"

Cadnan tried to find words, but there were no words. She
had won, and he knew it. He could not let Dara stay behind
to draw a great punishment, possibly even to die, to be no
more Dara. And there was no way of forcing her to go and
escape that fate—no way except to go with her.

"We must wait until they sleep," Dara said in a sudden return to practicality. "Then we go."

Cadnan looked around at the huddled, vaguely stirring forms of his companions. Fear was joined by a sort of sickness he had never known before. He was a slave, and that was good—but once outside where would he find work, or food, or a master? Where there was no master, Cadnan told himself, there was no slave. He was nothing, nameless, nonexistent.

But there was neither word nor action for him now. He tried once more to argue but his words were parried with a calm tenacity that left no room for discussion. In the end he was ready to do what he had to do—had to do in order, simply, to save Dara. There was no other reason. He needed none.

He had heard of the attraction of male for female, though some did not experience it until the true time of mating. He had not until that moment known how strong the attraction could be.

The waiting, though it seemed like positive days, didn't take long. The others in the room fell asleep, by habit, one by one, and soon Dara and Cadnan were the only ones left awake. Neither was tempted to sleep. Their own terror and their decision kept them very effectively alert.

Cadnan said: "If the masters see us?"

Dara turned on him a face that seemed completely calm. "They do not see us," she said flatly. "Now do not speak."

They rose and, silently, went to the door. The door opened just as quietly, and shut once again behind them.

The corridor was filled with watching eyes, Cadnan felt, but there were no masters in evidence. They stood for a second, waiting, and then Dara started down toward the big room at the end, her feet silent on the floor, and Cadnan followed her.

No masters were visible. There should have been guards, but the guards might have been anywhere. One escape had hardly served to alert a lazy, uninterested group who performed their duties out of no more than habit. Wherever the guards were resting, they were not in the corridor. Everything went smoothly. It was smoother than Cadnan was willing to believe.

Soon, though, they were actually in the great lobby of the building. It, too, was dark and empty. They stood dwarfed by the place, the gigantic doors that led to freedom no more than a few feet away.

Cadnan kept telling himself that where Marvor had gone he, too, could go. But Marvor had had a plan, and Cadnan had none.

Yet they were safe—so far, so far. They walked toward the door now, a step at a time. Each step seemed to take an hour, a full day. Dara walked ahead, straight and tall. Cadnan caught up with her, and she put out her hand. There was no more than an instant of hesitation. He took the hand.

That pledged them to each other, until the time of mating. But what was one more law now?

Another step. Another...

Cadnan, in the silence, was suddenly tempted to make a noise, any sort of noise—but it seemed impossible to create sound. The quiet dimness wrapped him like a blanket. He took another step.

Mating, he thought. If the chain of obedience was broken would the trees refuse to obey, in their turn? Puna had said so, and it was true. And if the trees refused to obey there would be no mating...

Yet Dara would be safe. That was the important thing. One thing at a time.

Another step...

And then, at last, the door.

Cadnan pushed at it, and it opened—and then there was sound, plenty of sound, more sound than he could have imagined, sound to fill the great lobby, to fill the entire building with rocking, trembling agonies of noise!

There was an alarm-bell, to be exact, an alarm-buzzer, combinations and solo cadenzas. The guards were, after all, no more than dressing. The automatic machinery never slept, and it responded beautifully and with enthusiasm.

Cadnan and Dara ran crazily out into the darkness. The building fell behind them and the jungle was ahead. Still they ran, but Cadnan felt the ground, bumpy instead of smooth, and stumbled once, nearly falling. He saw Dara ahead of him. Getting up and beginning again was automatic. Panic beat at him. The noise grew and grew. His feet moved, his heart thudded...

And then the lights went on.

Automatic sweep searchlights were keyed in. The machinery continued to respond.

Cadnan found himself suddenly struck blind. Ahead of him, Dara made a single, lonely, terrified sound that overrode all the alarms.

Cadnan tried to shout: "We must run! In the dark the masters cannot see—"

But, of course, by then it was too late to move.

The masters were all around them.

The escape was over.

CHAPTER FIFTEEN

OF COURSE THERE was Norma, Dodd told himself.

There was Norma to make everything worthwhile—except that Norma needed something, too, and he couldn't provide it. No one could provide it, not as long as no one was allowed off-planet. And it was quite certain, Dodd told himself gloomily, that the restrictions that had been in force yesterday were going to look like freedom and carefree joy compared with the ones going into effect tomorrow, or next week.

If, of course, there was going to be a tomorrow...that, he thought, was always in doubt. He managed sometimes to find a sort of illusory peace in thinking of himself as dead, scattered into component atoms, finished, forever unconscious, no longer wanting anything, no longer seeing the blinking words in his mind. Somewhere in his brain a small germ stirred redly against the prospect, but he tried to ignore it. That was no more than brute self-preservation, incapable of reasoning. That was no more than human nature.

And human nature, he knew with terror, was about to be overthrown once more.

It was only human, after all, to find the cheapest way to do necessary work. It was only human to want the profits high and the costs low. It was only human to look on other races as congenitally inferior, as less-than-man in any possible sense, as materials, in fact, to be used.

That was certainly human—centuries of bloody experience proved it. But the Confederation didn't want to recognize human nature. The Confederation didn't like slavery.

The rumor he'd heard from Norma was barely rumor any more. Instead, it had become the next thing to an officially announced fact. Everyone knew it, even if next to no one spoke of it. The Confederation was going to send ships—had probably sent ships already. There was going to be a war.

The very word "war" roused that red spark of self-preservation. It was harder, Dodd had found, to live with hope than to live without it. It was always possible to become resigned to a given state of affairs—but not if you kept thinking matters would improve. So he stamped on the spark, kept it down, ignored it. You had to accept things, and go on from there.

It was too bad Norma didn't know that.

He'd tried to tell her, of course. They'd even been talking, over in Building One, on the very night of the near-escape. He'd explained it all very clearly and lucidly, without passion (since he had cut himself off from hope he found he had very few passions of any kind left, and that made it easy); but she hadn't been convinced.

"As long as there's a fighting chance to live, I want to live," she'd said. "As long as there's any chance at all—the same as you."

"I know what I want," he told her grimly.

"What?" she asked, and smiled. "Do you like what you're doing? Do you like what I'm doing—what the whole arrangement is here?"

He shrugged. "You know I don't."

"Then get out of it," she said, still smiling. "You can, you know. It's easy. All you have to do is stop living—just like that! No more trouble."

"Don't be sil—"

"It can be done," she went on flatly. "There are hundreds of ways." Then the smile again. "But you'd rather live,

Johnny. You'd rather live, even this way, being a slaver, than put an end to it and to yourself."

He paused. "It's not the same thing."

"No," she said. "This way, you'd have to do the killing yourself. When the ships come, you can let them do it for you, just sit and wait for someone to kill you. Like a cataleptic. But you won't, Johnny."

"I will," he said.

She shook her head, the smile remaining. Her voice was quiet and calm, but there was a feeling of strain in it. There was strain everywhere, now. Everyone looked at the sky, and saw nothing. Everyone listened for the sound of engines, and there were no engines to hear. "Catalepsy is a kind of death, Johnny. And you'll have to inflict that much on yourself. You won't do it."

"You think I—" He stopped and swallowed, "You think I like living this way, don't you?"

"I think you like living," Norma said. "I think we all do, no matter how rough it gets. No matter how it grates on the nerves, or the flesh, of the supersensitive conscience. And I know how you feel, Johnny, I do—I—" She stopped very suddenly.

He heard his voice say: "I love you."

There was a silence.

"Johnny," she said, and her hands reached out for him blindly. He saw, incredibly, tears like jewels at the corners of her eyes. "Johnny—"

It was at that moment that the alarm-bell rang. It was heard only faintly in Building One, but that didn't matter. Dodd knew the direction, and the sound. He turned to go, for a second no more than a machine.

Norma's voice said: "Escape?"

He came back to her. "I—the alarm tripped off. This time they must have tried it through the front door, or a window. The last one must have tunneled through—"

He had to leave her. Instead he stood silently for a second. She said nothing.

"There are spots the steel's never covered," he said. "You can tunnel through if you're lucky." A pause. "I—"

"It's all right, Johnny," she said.

"Norma—"

"It's all right. I understand. It's all right."

Her voice. He hung on to it as he turned and walked away, found the elevator, started away from the room, the Building where she was, started off to do his duty.

His duty as a slaver.

The night was long, so long it could have been the night before the end of the world, the universe drawing one last deep breath before blowing out the candles and returning, at last, to peace and darkness and silence. Dodd spent it posted as one of the guards around the two cells where the Alberts were penned.

He had plenty of time to think.

And, in spite of Norma, in spite of everything, he was still sure of one thing. Because he was a slaver, because he acted, still, as a slaver and a master, hated by the Confederation, hated by the Alberts, hated by that small part of himself which had somehow stayed clean of the foulness of his work and his life, because of all that...

It was going to be very easy to die.

PUBLIC OPINION FOUR

Being an excerpt from a directive issued by the Executive and his Private Council, elected and confirmed by the Confederation, and upheld by majority vote of the Senate, the directive preserved in Confederation Archives, and signed under date of May 21 in the year two hundred and ten of the Confederation.

...It is therefore directed that sufficient ships be fitted out with all modern armaments, said fitting to be in the best judgment of the competent and assigned authorities, and dispatched without delay toward the planet known as Fruyling's World, both to subdue any armed resistance to Confederation policy, and to affirm the status of Fruyling's World as a Protectorate of the Confederation, subject to Confederation policy and Confederation judgment.

An act of this nature cannot be undertaken without grave thought and consideration. We affirm that such consideration has been given to this step.

It is needless to have fear as to the outcome of this action. No isolated world can stand against not only the might, but the moral judgment of the Confederation. Arms can be used only as a last resort, but times will come in the history of peoples when they must be so used, when no other argument is sufficient to force one party to cease and desist from immoral and unbearable practices.

In accordance with the laws of the Confederation, no weapons shall be used which destroy planetary mass.

In general, our efforts are directed toward as little bloodshed as possible. Our aim is to free the unfortunate native beings of Fruyling's World, and then to begin a campaign of re-education.

The fate of the human beings who have enslaved these natives shall be left to the Confederation Courts, which are competent to deal in such matters by statute of the year forty-seven of the Confederation. We pledge that We shall not interfere with such dealings by the Courts.

We may further reassure the peoples of the Confederation that no further special efforts on their part will be called for. This is not to be thought of as a war or even as a campaign, but merely as one isolated, regretted but necessary blow at a system which cannot but be a shock to the mind of civilized man.

That blow must be delivered, as We have been advised by Our Councilors. It shall be delivered.

The ships, leaving as directed, will approach Fruyling's World, leaving the FTL embodiments and re-entering the world-line, within ten days. Full reports will be available within one month.

In giving this directive, we have been mindful of the future status of any alien beings on worlds yet to be discovered. We hereby determine, for ourselves and our successors, that nowhere within reach of the Confederation may slavery exist, under any circumstances. The heritage of freedom that We have protected, and which belongs to all peoples, must be shared by all peoples everywhere, and to that end we direct Our actions, and Our prayers.

Given under date of May 21, in the year two hundred and ten of the Confederation, to be distributed and published everywhere within the Confederation, under Our hand and seal:

> Richard Germont
> by Grace of God Executive
> of the Confederation
> together with
> His Council in judgment assembled
> all members subscribing thereto.

CHAPTER SIXTEEN

THE ROOM HAD NO WINDOWS.
There was an air-conditioning duct, but Cadnan did not
know what such a thing was, nor would he have understood
without lengthy and tiresome explanations. He didn't know
he needed air to live. He knew only that the room was dark
and that he was alone, boxed in, frightened. He guessed that
somewhere, in another such room, Dara was waiting, just as
frightened as he was, and that guess made him feel worse.

Somehow, he told himself, he would have to escape.
Somehow he would have to get to Dara and save her from
the punishment, so that she did not feel pain. It was wrong
for Dara to feel pain.

But there was no way of escape. He had crept along the
walls, pushing with his whole body in hopes of some
opening. But the walls were metal and he could not push
through metal. He could, in fact, do nothing at all except sit
and wait for the punishment he knew was coming. He was
sure, now, that it would be the great punishment, that he and
Dara would be dead and no more. And perhaps, for his
disobedience, he deserved death.

But Dara could not die.

He heard himself say her name, but his voice sounded
strange and he barely recognized it. It seemed to be blotted
up by the darkness. And after that, for a long time, he said
nothing at all.

He thought suddenly of old Gornom, and of Puna. They
had said there was an obedience in all things. The slaves
obeyed, the masters obeyed, the trees obeyed. And, possibly,

the chain of obedience, if not already broken by Marvor's escape and what he and Dara had tried to do, extended also to the walls of his dark room. For a long time he considered what that might mean.

If the walls obeyed, he might be able to tell them to go. They would move and he could leave and find Dara. Since it would not be for himself but for Dara, such a command might not count as an escape. The chain of obedience might work for him.

This complicated chain of reasoning occupied him for an agonized time before he finally determined to put it to the test. But, when he did, the walls did not move. The door, which he tried as soon as it occurred to him to do so, didn't move either. With a kind of terror he told himself that the chain of obedience had been broken.

That thought was too terrible for him to contemplate for long, and he began to change it, little by little, in his mind. Perhaps (for instance) the chain was only broken for him and for Marvor. Perhaps it still worked as well as ever for all those who still obeyed the rules. That was better. It kept the world whole, and sane, and reasonable. But along with it came the picture of Gornom, watching small Cadnan sadly. Cadnan felt a weight press down on him, and grow, and grow.

He tried the walls and the door again, almost mechanically. He felt his way around the room. There was nothing he could do. But that idea would not stay in his mind. There had to be something, and he had to find it. In a few seconds, he told himself, he would find it. He tried the walls again. He was beginning to shiver. In a few seconds, only a few seconds, he would find the way, and then...

The door opened, and he whirled and stared at it. The sudden light hurt his eye, but he closed it for no more than a second. As soon as he could he opened it again, and stood, too unsure of himself to move, watching the master framed in the doorway. It was the one who was called Dodd.

Dodd stared back for what seemed a long time. Cadnan said nothing, waiting and wondering.

"It's all right," the master said at last. "You don't have to be afraid, Cadnan. I'm not going to hurt you." He looked sadly at the slave, but Cadnan ignored the look. There was no room in him for more guilt.

"I am not afraid," he said. He thought of going past Dodd to find Dara, but perhaps Dodd had come to bring him to her. Perhaps Dodd knew where she was. He questioned the master with Dara's name.

"The female?" Dodd asked. "She's all right. She's in another room, just like this one. A solitary room."

Cadnan shook his head. "She must not stay there."

"You don't have to worry," Dodd said. "Nobody's doing anything to her. Not right now, anyhow. I—not right now."

"She must escape," Cadnan said, and Dodd's sadness appeared to grow. He pushed at the air as if he were trying to move it all away.

"She can't." His hands fell to his sides. "Neither can you, Cadnan. I'm—look, there's a guard stationed right down the corridor, watching this door every second I'm here. There are electronic networks in the door itself, so that if you manage somehow to open it there'll be an alarm." He paused, and began again, more slowly. "If you go past me, or if you get the door open, the noise will start again. You won't get fifteen feet."

Cadnan understood some of the speech, and ignored the rest. It wasn't important. Only one thing was important: "She can not die."

Dodd shook his head. "I'm sorry," he said flatly. "There's nothing I can do." A silence fell and, after a time, he broke it. "Cadnan, you've really messed things up. I know you're right—anybody knows it. Slavery—slavery is—well, look, whatever it is, the trouble is it's necessary. Here and now. Without you, without your people, we couldn't last on this world. We need you, Cadnan, whether it's right or not—and that has to come first."

Cadnan frowned. "I do not understand," he said.

"Doesn't matter," Dodd told him. "I can understand how you feel. We've treated you—pretty badly, I guess. Pretty badly." He looked away with what seemed nervousness. But there was nothing to see outside the door, nothing but the corridor light that spilled in and framed him.

"No," Cadnan said earnestly, still puzzled. "Masters are good. It is true. Masters are always good."

"You don't have to be afraid of me," Dodd said, still looking away. "Nothing I could do could hurt you now—even if I wanted to hurt you. And I don't, Cadnan. You know I don't."

"I am not afraid," Cadnan said. "I speak the truth, no more. Masters are good. It is a great truth."

Dodd turned to face him. "But you tried to escape."

Cadnan nodded. "Dara can not die," he said in a reasonable tone. "She would not go without me."

"Die?" Dodd asked, and then, "oh, I see. The other—"

There was a long silence. Cadnan watched Dodd calmly. Dodd had turned again to stare out into the hallway, his hands nervously moving at his sides. Cadnan thought again of going past him, but then Dodd turned and spoke, his head low.

"I've got to tell you," he said. "I came here—I don't know why, but maybe I just came to tell you what's happening."

Cadnan nodded. "Tell me," he said, very calmly.

Dodd said: "I—" and then stopped. He reached for the door, held it for a second without closing it, and then, briefly, shook his head. "You're going to die," he said in an even, almost inhuman tone. "You're both going to die. For trying to escape. And the whole of your—clan, or family, or whatever that is—they're going to die with you. All of them." It was coming out in a single rush. Dodd's eyes fluttered closed. "It's my fault. It's our fault. We did it. We..."

And the rush stopped. Cadnan waited for a second, but there was no more. "Dara is not to die," he said.

Dodd sighed heavily, his eyes still closed. "I'm—sorry," he said slowly. "It's a silly thing to say. I'm sorry. I wish there was something I could do." He paused. "But there isn't. I wish—never mind. It doesn't matter. But you understand, don't you? You understand?"

Cadnan had room for only one thought, the most daring of his entire life. "You must get Dara away."

"I can't," Dodd said, unmoving.

Cadnan peered at him, half-fearfully. "You are a master." One did not give orders to masters, or argue with them.

But Dodd did not reach for punishment. "I can't," he said again. "If I help Dara, it's the jungle for me, or worse. And I can't live there. I need what's here. It's a matter of—a matter of necessity. Understand?" His eyes opened, bright and blind. "It's a matter of necessity," he said. "It has to be that way, and that's all."

Cadnan stared at him for a long second. He thought of Dara, thought of the punishment to come. The master had said there was nothing to do—but that thought was insupportable. There had to be something. There had to be a way...

There was a way.

Shouting: "Dara!" he found himself in the corridor, somehow having pushed past Dodd. He stood, turning, and saw another master with a punishment tube. Everything was still. There was no time for anything to move in.

He never knew if the tube had done it, or if Dodd had hit him from behind. Very suddenly, he knew nothing at all, and the world was blank, black, and distant. If time passed he knew nothing about it.

When he woke again he was alone again. He was back in the dark and solitary room.

CHAPTER SEVENTEEN

THE OFFICE WAS DIM NOW, at evening, but the figure behind the desk was rigid and unchanging, and the voice as singular as ever. "Do what you will," Dr. Haenlingen said. "I have always viewed love as the final aberration. It is the trap that lies in wait for the unwary sane. But no aberration is important, any more..."

"I'm trying to help him—" Norma began.

"You can't help him, child," Dr. Haenlingen said. Her eyes were closed. She looked as if she were preparing, at last, for death. "You feel too closely for him. You can't see him clearly enough to know what help he needs."

"But I've got to—"

"Nothing is predicated on necessity but action," Dr. Haenlingen said. "Certainly not success."

Norma went to the desk, leaned over it, looking down into the still, blank face. "It's too soon to give up," she said tensely. "You're just backing down, and there's no need for that yet—"

"You think not?" The face was still.

"There are lots of rumors, that's true," Norma said. "But—even if the worst comes to the worst—we have time. They aren't here yet. We can prepare—"

"Of course," the voice said. "We can prepare—as I am doing. There is nothing else for us, not any more. Idealism has taken over, and what we are and what we've done can go right on down the drain. Norma, you're a bright girl—"

"Too bright to sit around and do nothing!"

"But you don't understand this. Maybe you will, someday. Maybe I'll have a chance—but that's for later. Not now."

Norma almost reached forward to shake some sense into the old woman. But she was Dr. Haenlingen, after all

Norma's hand drew back again. "You can't just sit back and wait for them to come!"

"There is nothing else to do." The words were flat, echoless.

"Besides," Norma said desperately, "they're only rumors—"

She never finished her sentence. The blast rocked the room, and the window thrummed, steadied and then suddenly tinkled into pieces on the carpeted floor.

Norma was standing erect. "What's that?"

Dr. Haenlingen had barely moved. The eyes, in dimness, were open now. "That, my dear," the old woman said, "was your rumor."

"My—"

The blast was repeated. Ornaments on the desk rattled, a picture came off the far wall and thudded to the carpet. The air was filled with a fine dust and, far below, Norma could hear noise, a babble of voices...

"They're here!" she screamed.

Dr. Haenlingen sat very still, saying nothing. The eyes watched, but the voice made no comment. The hands were still, flat on the desk. Below, the voices continued—and then Dr. Haenlingen spoke.

"You'd better go," the calm voice said. "There will be others needing help—and you will be safer underground, in any case."

"But you—" Norma began.

"I may be lucky," Dr. Haenlingen said. "One of their bombs may actually kill me."

Her mouth open in an unreasoning accession of horror, Norma turned and fled. The third blast rattled the corridor as she ran crazily along it.

CHAPTER EIGHTEEN

DODD STAYED ON HIS POST because he had to. As a matter of fact, he hardly thought of leaving, or of doing anything at all. Minutes passed, and he stood in the hallway, quite alone. The other guard had spoken to him when Cadnan had been picked up and tossed back into solitary, but Dodd hadn't answered, and the guard had gone back to his own post. Dodd stood, hardly thinking, and waiting— though he could not have said what for.

This is the end. He had hit Cadnan. In those few seconds he had acted just as a good slaver was supposed to act. And that discovery shocked him. Even more than his response during the attempted escape, it showed him what he had become.

He had thought the words he used had some meaning. Now he knew they had next to none. They were only catch phrases, meant to make him feel a little better. He was a slaver, he had been trained as a slaver, and he would remain a slaver. What was it Norma had said?

"You'd rather live…"

It was true—it was all true. But there was (he told himself dimly) still, somewhere, hope the Confederation would come. When they did, he would die. He would die at last. And death was good, death was what he wanted…

No matter what Norma had told him, death was what he wanted.

He was still standing, those few thoughts expanding and filling his mind like water in a sponge, when the building, quite without warning, shook itself.

He heard the guard at the end of the corridor shouting. The building shook again, underneath and around him, dancing for a second like a man having a fit. Then he caught the first sounds of the bombardment.

"Norma!" He heard himself scream that one word over the sounds of blast and shout, and then he was out of the corridor, somehow, insanely, running across open ground. Behind him the alarms attached to the front doors of Building Three went off, but he hardly heard that slight addition to the uproar. God alone knew whether the elevators would be working…but they had to be, they had to stand up. After he found Building One (he could hardly trust the basement levels, choked by panic-stricken personnel from everywhere) he had to get an elevator and find Norma… He had to find Norma.

Overhead there was a flash and a dull roar. Dodd stared before him at a tangled, smoking mass of blackness. A second before, it had been a fringe of forest. Smoke coiled round toward him and he turned and ran for the side of Building Three. There were other sounds behind him, screams, shouts…

As he passed the Building the ground shook again and there was a sudden rise in the chorus of screams. He smelled acrid smoke, but never thought of stopping. The Building still stood gleaming in the bombardment flashes, and he went round the corner, behind it, and found himself facing the dark masses of One and Two, five hundred feet away over open ground.

As he watched there was a flash too bright for his eyes. He blinked and turned away, gasping. When he could look again a piece of Building Two was gone—looking, from five hundred feet distance, as if it had been bitten cleanly from the top, taking about four floors from the right side, taking the topmast, girders, and all…simply gone.

But that was Building Two, not Building One. Norma was still safe.

She had to be safe. He heaved in a breath of smoky air, and ran.

Behind him, around him, the bombardment continued.

PUBLIC OPINION FIVE

Being an excerpt from Chapter Seven of A Fourth Grade Reader in Confederation History, by Dr. A. Lindell Jones, with the assistance of Mary Beth Wilkinson, published in New York, U. S. A., Earth in September of the year one hundred and ninety-nine of the Confederation and approved for use in the public schools by the Board of Education (United) of the U. S. A., Earth, in January of the year two hundred of the Confederation.

...The first explorers on Fruyling's World named the new planet after the heroic captain of their ship, and prepared long reports on the planet for the scientists back home in the Confederation. The reports mentioned large metallic deposits, and this rapidly became important news.

The metallic deposits were badly needed by the Confederation for making many of the things which still are found in your homes: such useful objects as cleaners, whirlostats and such, all require metal from Fruyling's World.

Of course, there were not many explorers on the new planet, and it was a hard job for them to dig out the metal the Confederation needed.

But the planet had natives on it already. The natives were called Alberts, and here is a picture of them. Aren't they funny-looking?

The Alberts were happy to help with the digging in exchange for some of the good things the explorers talked about, because they didn't have many good things. But the explorers built houses for them and gave them food and taught them English, and the Alberts dug in the ground and helped get the metal ready to ship back to the Confederation.

...The following list of Review Questions may be helpful to the instructor:

1. Why is Fruyling's World called by that name? After whom was it named?
2. What is so valuable about Fruyling's World?
3. Who helps the explorers dig up the metal?
4. Why do they help?

CHAPTER NINETEEN

FOR CADNAN, the time passed slowly.

Consciousness came back, along with a thudding ache in the head and a growing hunger. However, there were no leaves on the smooth metal of the floor, and the demands of his body had to be ignored. His mind began to drift. Once he heard a voice, but when he told himself that the voice was not real, it went away. He found his hands moving as if he were pushing the buttons of his job. He stopped them and in a second they were moving again.

Then the room itself began to shake.

Cadnan had no doubts of his sanity. This was different from the imaginary voice. The room shook again and he wondered whether this were some new sort of punishment. But it did not hurt him.

The rumbling sound of the bombardment came to him only dimly, and for brief seconds. To Cadnan, it sounded like a great machine, and he wondered about that, too, but he could find no answers.

The rumbling came again, and sounded nearer. Cadnan thought of machines shaking his small room, perhaps making it hot as the machines made metal hot. If that happened, he knew, he would die.

He called: "Dara." It was hard to hear his own voice. There was no answer, and he had expected none—but he had needed to call.

The rumbling came again. Surely, he told himself, this was a new punishment, and it was death.

There was only one thing for him to do. He sat cross-legged on the smooth floor as the rumble and the other sounds continued, and in opposition to them he made his song, chanting in a loud and even voice. He had learned that a song was to be made when facing death. He had learned that in the birth huts, and he did not question it.

The song was necessary, and his voice, carrying over the sounds that filtered through to him, was clear and strong.

"I am Cadnan,

"I am Cadnan of Bent Line Tree,

"I work for the masters,

"I push buttons and the machine obeys me,

"I push buttons when the masters say to do it.

"My song is short. I am near the dead.

"I have broken the chain, the chain of obedience.

"I do not want to break this chain.

"I must break it. Dara says I go.

"If I do not go then Dara does not go.

"Dara must go. I break the chain.

"For this I am near the dead and the room shakes.

"It is my death and my song.

"I am Cadnan and Bent Line Tree and I work."

After the song was over, he remained sitting, waiting for what had to come. The rumbling continued, and the room shook more strongly. For some seconds he waited, and then he was standing erect, because he could see.

The door, sprung from its lock by the shaking of the building, had fallen a little open. As Cadnan watched, it opened a bit more, and he went and pushed at it. Under a very light shove, it swung fully open, and the corridor, lights flickering down its length, stood visible. As Cadnan peered out, the lights blinked off, and then came on again.

The rumbling was very loud now, but he saw no machines. He went into the corridor in a kind of curious daze. There were no masters anywhere, none to watch or hurt him. He called once more for Dara, but now he could not hear himself at all. The rumbling was only one of the sounds that battered at him dizzily. There were bells and buzzes, shrieks and cascades of brutal, grinding sounds more powerful than could be made by any machine Cadnan could imagine.

He started down the corridor. The masters had taken Dara in that direction, opposite to his own. Suddenly, one of his own kind stood before him, and he recognized a female, Hortat, through the dusty air. Hortat was staring at him with a frozen expression in her eye.

"What is it?" she asked. "What happens?"

Cadnan, without brutality, brushed her aside. "I do not know. The masters know. Wait and they tell you." He did not consider whether the statement were true, or false, or perhaps (under these new circumstances) entirely meaningless. It was a noise he had to make in order to get Hortat out of his way. She stood against the corridor wall as he passed, watching him.

He went on past her, moving faster now, into the central room from which corridors radiated. The lights went off again and then came on. He peered round but there were no masters. Besides, he thought, if the masters found him the worst they could do would be to kill him, and that was unimportant now. He already had his song.

In a corridor at the opposite side of the central room he saw a knot of Alberts, among whom he recognized only Puna. The elder was speaking with some others, apparently trying to calm them. Cadnan pushed his way to Puna's side and heard the talk die down, while all stared at the audacious newcomer.

"I am looking for Dara," Cadnan said loudly, to be heard over the continuous noise from elsewhere.

Puna said: "I do not know Dara," and turned away.

Another shouted: "Where are the masters? Where is

work?"

Cadnan shouted: "Wait for the masters," and went on, pushing his way through the noise, through the babbling crowd of Alberts. There were no masters visible anywhere. That was a new thing and a strange one, but too many new things were happening. Cadnan barely noticed one more.

At the front of his mind now was only the thought of Dara. Behind that was a vague, nagging fear that he was the cause of all the rumbling and shaking of the building, and all else, by his breaking of the chain of obedience. Now, he told himself, the buildings even did not obey.

Then he heard a voice say, "Cadnan," and all other thought fled. The voice was hers...Dara's. He saw her ahead and went to her quickly.

She had not been hurt.

That fact sent a wave of relief through him, a wave so strong that for a second he could barely stand.

"The door opens," she said when he had reached her, in a small and frightened voice. "The masters are not here."

"They return," Cadnan said, but without complete assurance. In this barrage of novelty, who could make any statement certain?

Dara nodded. "Then we must go," she said. "If they are not here, then maybe they do not hear the noise when we open the door—and there is much noise already to hide it. Maybe they do not see us."

"And if they do?"

Dara looked away. "I have my song," she said. "And I have mine." It was settled.

As they headed toward the big front doors others followed, but there was no use bothering about that. When Cadnan opened the door, in fact, the others fell back and remained, staring, until it had shut behind them. There was the great noise of bells and buzzers—but that had been going on, Cadnan realized, even before they had begun. Outside, the spotlights seemed weaker. There was smoke everywhere, and ahead the forest was a black and frightening mass.

He looked at Dara, who showed her fear for one instant.

"I am also afraid," he told her, and was rewarded by a look of gratitude. "But we must go on." He took her hand.

They walked slowly into the smoke and the noise. As they reached the edge of the forest, the sound began to diminish, very slowly; and, ahead of them, through the haze and beyond the twisted trees, the sun began to rise.

They walked for a long while, and by the time they had finally stopped the noise was gone. There was a haze over everything, but through the haze a morning sun shone, and a heavy peace hung over the world.

There were trees, but these were neither like Bent Line Tree, for mating, nor for food. Perhaps, Cadnan thought, they were for building, but he did not know, and had no way to know until an elder showed him.

And there were no elders any more. There were neither elders nor masters, there was only Cadnan, and Dara—and, somewhere—Marvor and the group he had spoken of. Cadnan peered round, but he saw no one. There were small new sounds, and those were frightening, but they were so tiny—rustles, squeaks, no more—that Cadnan could not feel greatly frightened by them.

The green-gray light that filtered through the trees and haze bathed both Alberts in a glow that enhanced their own bright skin-color. They stood for a few seconds, listening, and then Dara turned.

"I know these sounds," she said, "I talk to others in our room, and some of these work outside. They tell me of these sounds and this place. It is called a jungle."

Cadnan made a guess. "The trees make the sound."

"Small beings make it," Dara corrected him. "There are such small beings, not slaves and not masters. They have no speech but they make sound."

Cadnan meditated on this new fact for a short time. Then Dara spoke again.

"Where is Marvor? The time of mating is near."

Cadnan saw her meaning. It was necessary to find Bent Line Tree, or some like it, and advising elders, all before the time of mating. Yet he did not know how. "Maybe masters come," he suggested hopefully, "and tell us what to do."

Dara shook her head. "No. The masters kill us. They do not lead us any more. Only we lead ourselves."

Cadnan thought privately that such an idea was silly, almost too silly for words. How could a person lead himself? But he said nothing to Dara, not wanting to hurt her. Instead, he pretended, helplessly, to agree with her: "You are right. We lead ourselves now."

"But we must know where Marvor stays."

That sounded more reasonable. Cadnan considered it for a minute. Wherever Marvor was hiding, it had to be somewhere in the jungle. And so, in order to find him, they had only to walk through it.

And so they set out—on a walk long enough to serve as an aboriginal Odyssey for the planet. The night-beasts, soft glowing circles of eyes and mouths which none of their race had ever seen before—the giant flesh-eating plants; the herd of bovine monsters which, confused, stampeded at them, shaking the ground with their tread and making the feathery trees shake as if there were a hurricane. All this might have made an epic, had there been anyone to record it. But Cadnan expected no more and no less. The world was strange. Any piece of it was as strange as any other.

Once they came across a grove of food-trees, and ate their fill, but they saved little to take with them, being unused to doing their own planning. So they went on, hungry and in the midst of dangers scarcely recognized, sleeping at night however they could, travelling aimlessly by day. And after a time that measured about three days they stopped in a small clearing and heard a voice.

"Who is there?"

Cadnan, frightened by the sudden noise, managed to say, "I am Cadnan and there is one with me called Dara. We look for Marvor."

The strange voice hesitated a second, but its words, when it did speak, were in a tone that was peaceful enough.

"I know of Marvor and will take you to him. It is not far to where he stays."

CHAPTER TWENTY

AFTER THE FIRST RUSH OF BATTLE, matters began to quiet a little. Against tremendous odds, and in a few brief hours, the armaments of Fruyling's World had managed to beat off the Confederation fleets, and these had withdrawn to reform and to prepare for a new phase of the engagement.

In the far-off days before the age of Confederation, war had, perhaps, been an affair of grinding, constant attack and defense. No one could say for sure. Many records were gone, much had been destroyed. But now there was waiting, preparation, linked batteries of armaments and calculators for prediction—and then the brief rush and flurry of battle, followed by the immense waiting once more.

For Dodd, it was a time to breathe and to look around. He had enough work to do. The damage to Building Three, and the confusion among the Alberts, had to be dealt with, and all knew time was short. Very few of the Alberts had actually escaped—and most of those, Dodd told himself bitterly, would die in their own jungles, for lack of knowledge or preparation. Most, though, simply milled around, waiting for the masters, wondering and worrying.

Norma was safe, of course. After a frantic search Dodd had found her below ground in the basements of Building One, along with most of the Psych division. Without present duties forcing them to guard or maintain the Alberts, the Psych division had holed up almost entire in the steel corridors that echoed with the dull booms of the battle. He'd gasped out some statement of relief, and Norma had smiled at him.

"I knew you'd be safe," she said. "I knew you had to be."

And of course she was right. Even if what she said had sounded cold, removed—he had to remember she was under shock, too, the attack had come unexpectedly on them all. It didn't matter what she said. She was safe. He was glad of that.

Of course he was, he thought. Of course he was.

Even if the things she said, the cold-blooded way she looked at the world, sometimes bothered him...

And, a day later, when everyone was picking up the scattered pieces of the world and attempting, somehow, to rig a new defense, she'd said more. Not about herself, or about him. Tacitly, they knew all of that had to wait for a conclusion to the battle. But about the Alberts...

"Of course they're not disloyal," she told him calmly. "They don't even know what disloyalty means. We've seen to that. The masters are as much a part of their world as—as food, I suppose. You don't stage a rebellion against food, do you?"

Dodd frowned. "But some of them have escaped."

"Wandered, you mean. Just wandered off. And—oh, I suppose a few have. Our methods aren't perfect. But they are pretty good, Johnny. Look at the number of Alberts who simply stayed around."

"We're making them slaves."

"No." She shook her head, violently. "Nobody can make a slave. All we've done is seize an opportunity. Think of our own history, Johnny. First the clan, or the band—some sort of extended family group. Then, when real leadership is needed, the slave-and-master relationship."

"Now, wait a minute," Dodd said. Norma had been brainwashed into some silly set of slogans. It was his job to break them down. "The clan can elect leaders—"

"Sure it can," she said. "But democracy is a civilized

commodity, Johnny—in a primitive society it's a luxury the society can't afford. What guarantees have you got that the clan will elect the best possible leader? Or that, having elected him, they'll follow him along the best paths?"

"Self-interest—"

But again she cut him off. "Self-interest is stupid," she said casually. "A child needs to learn. Schooling is in the best interest of that child. Agreed?"

"Yes, but—"

"Did you ever hear of a child who liked school, Johnny?" she asked. "Did you ever hear of a child who went to school, regularly, eagerly, without some sort of force being applied, physical, mental or moral? No, Johnny, self-interest is short sighted. Force is all that works."

"But—" He was sure she was wrong, but he couldn't see where. "Who are we to play God for them?" he said at last.

"They need somebody," Norma said. "And we need them. Even."

She seemed harder now, somehow, more decided. Dodd saw that the one attack had changed a lot—in Norma, in everyone. Albin, for instance, wasn't involved with fun any more. He had turned into a fanatical drill-sergeant, with a squad of Alberts under him, and it was even rumored that he slept in their quarters.

And Norma...what had happened to her? After the fighting was over, and they could talk again, could relax and reach out for each other once again.

She had become so hard.

One new fear ran through the defenders. The Alberts who had escaped might return, some said, vowing vengeance against the masters...

CHAPTER TWENTY-ONE

CADNAN HAD LEARNED much in a very short time. Everyone was hurried now, as the time of mating approached more and more quickly and as the days sped by. Knowledge was thrown at Cadnan and at Dara in vast, indigestible lumps, and they were left to make what they could of it, while the others went about their normal assigned work.

He learned about the invasion, for instance—or as much about it as Marvor, the elders and a few other late arrivals could piece together. Their explanations made surprisingly good sense in the main, though none of them, not even Marvor, could quite comprehend the notion of masters having masters above them. It appeared contrary to reason.

Cadnan learned, also, the new trees in this new place, which the elders had found. There were food trees nearby, and others whose leaves were meant for building, and there were also trees of mating like his own Bent Line Tree. No one could tell Cadnan where Bent Line Tree itself might be, and so he became resigned to his first mating with a new tree, which the elders had called Great Root Tree. It was not truly right, he told himself, but there was nothing to do about it.

The life in the jungle made Cadnan uncomfortable. He was nothing larger than himself, and he felt very small. When he had masters, he was a part of something great, of the chain of obedience. But here, in the jungle, there was no chain (and would the trees obey when their time came?) and each felt himself alone. It was not good to feel alone, Cadnan decided; yet, again, there was nothing he could do. It mattered for a time, and then it ceased to matter.

The time of mating came closer and closer, and Cadnan felt his own needs grow with the hours. The sun rose, and fell, and rose again.

Then the time came.

It was dark. There were others near them, but they were alone. Cadnan knew Dara was standing near him in the darkness, though he saw nothing. He heard her breath coming slowly at first, and then a little faster. He did not hear his own, but that was no matter. There was a sound from a small night-animal, but it did not come near. He stood, with Dara, near to Great Root Tree. If he put out his hand, he could touch it.

But he kept his hand at his side. Touching the tree, at that moment, was wrong. There were the old rules, the true rules, and to think of them made him feel better.

Dara said nothing. It was not necessary for her to speak. They knew each other, and the attraction was very strong. Cadnan had felt the attraction before, but until that moment he had not known how strong it was. And then it grew, and grew.

Still they did not move. Darkness covered both, and there was no more sound. The very feeling of the presence of others disappeared. There was nothing but Cadnan, and Dara, and Great Root Tree.

It called to him, but not to him alone. He knew what he had to do. He felt the front of his body growing warm and then hot. He felt the first touch of the liquid.

He touched Dara. Their fronts touched. That alone was more than Cadnan had ever imagined yet it was not enough. Still there was more he was called on to do. He did not think about it, or know of it until it was done. He moved against Dara, as she against him. He was not himself. He was more and less, he was only the front of his body and he was Great

Root Tree, he was all trees, all worlds...

When he stepped back it was like dying, but he could not die, since there was more for him to do. He stood still, very close to Dara, and, remaining close, he went to the tree. It was not far and both knew the path, but it seemed far. Cadnan could feel the mixed liquids on his front, his and Dara's. Great Root Tree seemed to call these liquids to itself, and himself and Dara with them.

They walked to it. In the darkness they could not see it, but they knew the tree. They had spent time knowing it before that night. Cadnan reached out a slow hand and touched the back of the tree, almost as smooth as metal, with only minute irregularities throughout its surface. Once again a long time seemed to pass, but it was not long.

Then he was against the tree while Dara stood behind, waiting. He pressed himself against the bark and he felt himself becoming part of Great Root Tree, becoming the tree itself; and this lasted for all time and no time, and he was separated from it and saw Dara come to where he had pressed, and move delicately and then fiercely upon the bark; then he saw nothing but heard her breathing faster and faster, and all sound stopped...there was a long silence...and then her breathing began again, very slowly, very slowly.

She returned to Cadnan and took his hand. It was finished. Soon the tree would bud with the results of the liquids rubbed on it. After that, there would be small ones, and Cadnan would be an elder. All of this was in the future and it was very dim in Cadnan's mind, but everything was dim. He lay on the ground and Dara lay near him, both very tired, too tired to think of anything, and he felt himself shaking for a time and his breath hissed in and out until the shaking stopped.

Dara, too, was quiet at last. The darkness had not changed. There was no sound, and no motion.

It was over.

CHAPTER TWENTY-TWO

WHEN THE Confederation forces reformed, they came on with a crash. Dodd had heard for months that Fruyling's World could never stand up to a real assault. He had even thought he believed it. But the first attack had bolstered his gloomy confidence, and the results of the second came not only as a surprise but as a naked shock.

The Alberts in spite of a few fearful masters, had been issued Belbis tubes and fought valiantly with them; the batteries did everything expected of them, and the sky was lit with supernal flashes of blinding color throughout one hard-fought night. Dodd himself, carrying a huge Belbis beam, braced himself against the outer wall of Building One and played the beam like a hose on any evidence of Confederation ships up there in the lightning-lit sky. He felt only like a robot, doing an assigned and meaningless job, and it was only later that he realized he had been shivering all the time he had used the killing beam. As far as he could tell he had hit nothing at all.

The battle raged for six hours, and by its end Dodd was half-deafened by the sound and half-blinded by the sporadic rainbow flashes that meant a hit or a miss or a return-blow, lancing down from the ships to shake buildings and ground. At first he had thought of Norma, safe in the bunkers below Building One. Then she had left his mind entirely and there was only the battle, the beginning of all things and the end— only the battle and the four constant words in his mind. Even when the others began to retreat and Dodd heard the shouted orders he never moved. His hands were frozen to the Belbis beam, his ears heard only battle and his eyes saw only the shining results of his own firing.

There was a familiar voice—Albin's. "...get out while you've got a chance—it's over..."

Another voice: "...better surrender than get killed..."

The howls of a squad of Alberts as a beam lanced over them, touching them only glancingly, not killing but only subjecting them to an instant of "punishment"; and the howls ceased, swallowed up in the greater noise.

A voice: "...Johnny..."

It meant nothing. Dodd no longer knew he had a name. He was only an extension of his beam, firing with hypnotized savagery into the limitless dark.

"Johnny..."

He heard his own voice answering. "Get back to the bunker. You'll be safe in the bunker. Leave me alone." His voice was strange to his ears, like an echo of the blasts themselves, rough and loud.

Dawn was beginning to color the sky, very slightly. That was good. In daylight he might be able to see the ships. He would fire the beam and see the ships die. That was good, though he hardly knew why. He knew only that it pleased him. He watched the dawn out of a corner of one eye.

"Johnny, it's all over, we've lost, it's finished. Johnny, come with me."

Norma's voice. But Norma was in the bunker. Norma had caused the battle. She had made the slaves. Now she was safe while he fought. The thought flickered over his mind like a beam blast, and sank into blackness.

"Johnny, please...Johnny...come on, now. Come on. You'll be safe. You don't want to die..."

No, of course he didn't. He fired the beam, aimed, fired again, aimed again. He could die when his enemies were dead. He could die when everyone who was trying to kill him was dead. Then he could die, or live. It made no difference.

He fired again, aimed again, fired...

"Johnny, please..." The voice distracted him a little. No wonder he couldn't kill all the ships, with that voice distracting him. It went on and on: "Johnny, you don't have to die...you're not responsible...Johnny, you aren't a slaver, you just had a job to do. Killing isn't the answer, Johnny, death isn't the answer..."

The voice went on and on, but he tried to ignore it. He had to keep firing—that was his job, and more than his job. It was his life. It was all of his life that he had left.

Dr. Haenlingen had told her she was too close to see properly, and, of course, she was. Perhaps she knew that, in the final seconds. Perhaps she never did. But that Dodd, who wanted to die and who considered death the only proper atonement for his life, could have displaced that wish onto the Confederation, onto his "enemies," and so reached a precarious and temporary balance, never occurred to her. And if it had, perhaps she could have done nothing better...time had run out.

Time had run out. Johnny Dodd's enemies wanted him dead, and so he had to kill them (and so avoid killing himself, and so avoid recognizing how much he himself wanted to be dead). But the balance wasn't complete. There was still the guilt, still the terrible guilt that made it right for the Confederation to kill him.

The guilt had to be displaced, too.

Norma did what she could, did what she thought right. "You don't have to die," she told him. "You're not responsible."

That was what he heard, and it was enough. He hadn't made the Alberts into slaves. He hadn't made the Alberts into slaves.

But he knew who had. Long before, it had all been carefully explained to him. All of the tricks that had been used...

Of course, Dodd thought. Of course he wasn't responsible.

He felt an enormous peace descend on him, like a cloak, as he turned with the beam in his hand and smiled at Norma. She began, tentatively, to return his smile.

The beam cut her down where she stood and left a swathe of jungle behind her black and smoking.

Dodd, his job completed, dropped the beam. For one instant four words lit up in his mind, and then everything went out into blankness and peace. The body remained, the body moved, the body lived, for a time. But after those four words, blinding and bright and then—swallowed up—Johnny Dodd was gone.

He had found what he needed.

This is the end.

PUBLIC OPINION SIX

From A Cultural Record of Fruyling's World
Personal Histories of the Natives (called Alberts)
As Dictated and Preserved on Tape by Historical Commission HN3-40-9
Subject (called) Cadnan

...Dara is dead in the returning, when new masters come to us and say the fighting is over. It is an accident that kills her, a stumble, they say, against a plant that is dangerous to animal life and to our kind. The accident is over and Dara is dead, and we return.

I find Marvor after the fighting, once only, and I ask him what it is that is so important about this fighting. The

Confederation—the masters we now have—are only masters like the ones we know. Marvor looks at me with a look as if he, too, is a master.

"Freedom is that important," he says. "Freedom is the most important thing."

I know that Marvor is not right, because I know the most important thing—it is the dead. For me Dara is most important, and I remember Puna, who is dead in the fighting. The rest does not matter. I say this now, knowing that the talk-machine hears me and that the Confederation hears me.

I say: "Can freedom make me feel happy?"

Marvor looks more like a master. "Freedom is good," he says

"And yet Dara is dead," I say. "And others are dead. How do I feel happy when I know this?"

"In freedom," Marvor tells us, "Dara would be safe, and the others."

"Yet it is freedom that kills them," I say.

Marvor says: "Not freedom but the war. The fight against our masters here, the old masters, to make them give us freedom."

I say: "Do not our old masters have freedom?"

"They do," Marvor says, "now."

This puzzles me. I say: "But they have freedom at all times. They have what they want, and if freedom is a good, and they want it, then they have it."

Marvor says: "It is true. They have freedom for themselves."

"Yet these other masters tell them what to do," I say, "and fight them to make them do it. This is not the freedom you tell of."

Marvor says: "There is a difference."

I do not see this difference, and he can not tell it to me though he tries hard. But I think maybe the new masters can tell me what it is. Marvor is going to what they call a school and I also go. This is a place where masters tell things, and we must remember them. Remembering is not hard, but we must think also, and do work. It is not enough to ask a question and find an answer. It is necessary to find our own answers.

A master asks us to count, and then to do things with the numbers we use in our counting. This is called arithmetic. We must do things with the numbers every day, and if we do not the masters are not happy with us. This arithmetic is hard—it is all new. Yet if I do it right I do not find more food or a better place or any thing I want. I do not see what is the use of this arithmetic.

But the use does not matter. The master tells me a use. He says arithmetic and all of the things in the school raise the cultural level. I do not know what a cultural level is or if it is good to be raised. The masters do not care whether I know this. They make me do what they want me to do.

And it is not simple like pushing buttons and watching a machine. It is not simple like all the things I do since I am small Cadnan. It is hard—very hard—and all the time it is more hard.

Every day there is a school. Every day there is hard work. Marvor says that freedom means doing for yourself what you want and deciding right and wrong. I say freedom is bad because the masters know right and wrong and we do not. Others say with me. There are some who know the old truths and think it is better when we, too, can understand right and wrong.

But the masters say what we have is freedom. I say it is not so. The masters tell us what to do. They tell us to do arithmetic, to do all other school things, and we do not do for ourselves what we want. We do not do anything for ourselves, but always the masters tell us.

This is the same as before the fighting. It is always the same. A master is a master.

But the old masters were the best. I remember the old masters and the old work, and I want this time to come again. I want the old work, which is easy, and not this new work, which is hard. I want the old slavery, where we know right and wrong, and not the new slavery, where only the masters know and they say they cannot tell us.

If am free, if I can decide for myself what it is that I want, then this is what I decide.

I want the old masters back again.

I, Cadnan, say this.

PUBLIC OPINION SEVEN

From the speech of Dr. Anna Haenlingen
Before the High Court (Earth) of the Confederation
Preparatory to the Passing of Sentence

...The attorneys for the Confederation government have called our position cynical, and my own attorneys have attempted, without success, to refute this charge. As head of the Psychological Division on Fruyling's World previous to the unjustified intervention of Confederation force in the affairs of that world, I feel it incumbent on me to define a position which even our own advocates do not seem to understand.

I bear a good deal of the responsibility for conditions on Fruyling's World, and I have not shirked that responsibility. I found the natives of that world in a condition of slavery, due to the work of my predecessors. I maintained them in that slavery, and made no move whatever to free them or to mitigate their status.

This is, in truth, a cynical position. I do not believe, and I have never believed, that freedom is necessarily a good for all people at all times. Like any other quality, it can be used for good or for evil.

In the contact between any barbarian people and any civilized people, some species of slavery is necessary. The barbarian does not know that he is a barbarian, and the only way to convey to him the fact that he stands at the bottom of a long ladder—a ladder so long that we have by no means reached its end, and have perhaps not yet seen its midpoint—is to force him to make contact with elements of civilization, and to utilize continuous force to keep this contact alive and viable.

The alien—the barbarian—will not of himself continue contact in any meaningful manner. The gap is too great between his life and that of the civilized person, and a disparity so great becomes, simply, invisible. Under conditions of equality, the civilized person must degenerate to barbarian status. His mind can comprehend the barbarian, and he can move in that direction. The barbarian, incapable of comprehension of the civilized world, cannot move toward that which he cannot see.

In order to bring him into motion, slavery and subjection appear necessities. There has been no civilization of which we have record that has not passed through a period of subjection to another, more forceful civilization: the Greeks, the Romans, the Jews, all the great civilizations of which there is available record have passed through a period of slavery. Nor is this accidental.

Some force must be applied to begin the motion toward civilization. That force—disguise it how you will—is slavery. It is clearly the attempt to make another person do what he would not do, does not wish to do, and sees no personal profit in doing, under threat of punishment. It is subjection. That subjection is all we mean by slavery.

And slavery is a necessity.

Perhaps we were wrong. Perhaps the slavery that was dictated to us by the conditions that prevailed upon Fruyling's World was not the best sort available. But freedom is not, in any case, the answer. A man may die as the result of too much oxygen. A culture, likewise, may die of too much freedom.

I have no fear of the sentence of this court. My death is unimportant, and I do not fear it. I might fear that my work be left undone, were I not certain that, under whatever name, the Confederation will find it necessary to maintain slavery on Fruyling's World.

Of this, I am quite sure.

From the Report of Genmo. Darad Farnung, Commanding Confederation Expeditionary Force, 3rd Sector From Base of Occupation, Fruyling's World (NC34157:495:4)

...In the three planetary months (approx. ninety-two Solar days) since occupation of this world, no serious incidents have been reported. The previous "rulers" of this world have been transshipped to Earth for disposal there by Confederation governmental process. With the introduction of fully automated machinery, the world's primary resources are being utilized for the good of the Confederation without the introduction of any form of slavery or forced labor whatever...

...Regarding education and aid as involving the native population, the initial shipments of teachers, investigators and experts in xenopsychology have enabled the occupation force to begin a full educational program for the benefit of the natives. This program has been accepted by the natives without delay and without any untoward incidents, and reports to the contrary are assumed to have been initiated by disaffected personnel. The program of education in a democratic and workable form of government for these natives is, and must remain, one of the shining examples of the liberative effects of Confederation doctrine and government, and should provide a valuable precedent in future cases...

...Reports that the profits of the major business of this world, since the introduction of automated machinery and experts for the repair and upkeep thereof, have decreased to the vanishing point should not be taken as serious. This is assumed to be merely a temporary hardship due to the transfer workload from the natives to the automated structure... Since the only alternative is the placement of the workload on enslaved natives of this world, the temporary rise in taxes due to the loss on essential product profit should be taken as a needed and welcome sacrifice in the name of liberty by the peoples of the Confederation...

...A list of further urgent materials, together with a list of specialties now urgently required in order to maintain full production here, and a revised schedule of budgetary requirements to include these additional requisitions, is hereby appended...

THE END

If you've enjoyed this book, you will not want to miss these terrific titles...

ARMCHAIR SCI-FI & HORROR DOUBLE NOVELS, $12.95 each

D-11   **PERIL OF THE STARMEN** by Kris Neville
           THE FORGOTTEN PLANET by Murray Leinster

D-12   **THE STAR LORD** by Boyd Ellanby
           CAPTIVES OF THE FLAME by Samuel R. Delany

D-13   **MEN OF THE MORNING STAR** by Edmond Hamilton
           PLANET FOR PLUNDER by Hal Clement and Sam Merwin, Jr.

D-14   **ICE CITY OF THE GORGON** by Chester S. Geier and Richard Shaver
           WHEN THE WORLD TOTTERED by Lester del Rey

D-15   **WORLDS WITHOUT END** by Clifford D. Simak
           THE LAVENDER VINE OF DEATH by Don Wilcox

D-16   **SHADOW ON THE MOON** by Joe Gibson
           ARMAGEDDON EARTH by Geoff St. Reynard

D-17   **THE GIRL WHO LOVED DEATH** by Paul W. Fairman
           SLAVE PLANET by Laurence M. Janifer

D-18   **SECOND CHANCE** by J. F. Bone
           MISSION TO A DISTANT STAR by Frank Belknap Long

D-19   **THE SYNDIC** by C. M. Kornbluth
           FLIGHT TO FOREVER by Poul Anderson

D-20   **SOMEWHERE I'LL FIND YOU** by Milton Lesser
           THE TIME ARMADA by Fox B. Holden

ARMCHAIR SCIENCE FICTION CLASSICS, $12.95 each

C-4   **CORPUS EARTHLING**
       by Louis Charbonneau

C-5   **THE TIME DISSOLVER**
       by Jerry Sohl

C-6   **WEST OF THE SUN**
       by Edgar Pangborn

ARMCHAIR SCI-FI & HORROR GEMS SERIES, $12.95 each

G-1   **SCIENCE FICTION GEMS, Vol. One**
       Isaac Asimov and others

G-2   **HORROR GEMS, Vol. One**
       Carl Jacobi and others